Published by REGI Books, a Subsidiary of Rogers
Entertainment Group International.

For information, please contact:
d. E. Rogers at: nextgreatwriter@gmail.com
www.BlackStatesofAmerica.com

ISBN: 978-1-64970-847-2
Printed in the United States of Sea Islands

Black States
of
America

Dedication

The lives of black people in America has always been filled with challenges and obstacles to overcome. Carrying tears of a broken family tree that when traced back stops at a person in a ledger listed by their first name only. Unlike any other race, the roadblocks black people have faced have been long and damaging to the mind and soul. The same way generational wealth creates access and elitism, generational poverty and pain creates hopelessness and closed doors. With over 400 years of being in this country called America, most of our time has been spent living the American Nightmare while others have been dreaming. The 2nd, 3rd, and 4th class citizen status are a slap in the face. Just like the go back to Africa chants, but through it all we have survived and stood tall. We may bend at times, but never have we been broken. Our spirit of a great tomorrow has never wavered, but as we reflect on black treatment, stereotypes, police brutality, and inequality, we can no longer silently wait for tomorrow. Today is our rally call for real change. Through all the suppressing years of slavery and thereafter, black people have had a glimpse of what our greatness could be. Creating technology, innovations in medicine, and becoming superior in creativity and athleticism to name a few, we have shown the world our true power, but the world still wants to suppress us.

When you see that rose crushing through the concrete think of the life of the average black person trying to make it in this country. Knowing our power and heart filled spirit was the motivation behind me writing this novel. In my heart, I know the keys to achieving true equality is through wealth and ownership and if Lincoln had lived to see Special Field Order Number 15 fulfilled, the black people you see today would be less dependent on others to hear our voice because we would own our voice and control our narrative. Though this is fiction, I want my readers to read and understand that we cannot have just one person at the top of the mountain unless that person is lifting others up to join them. I dedicate this book to the ones gone, the ones still fighting, and the ones that will carry the torch in the future. Much love to you and all humankind.

Black States
of
America

By d. E. Rogers

door, stepped forward, and shot Major Rathbone from behind with a Derringer "one shot" pistol, thinking it was President Lincoln.

As the gunsmoke cleared and Major Rathbone slumped over in his chair and fell backward, Booth's and Lincoln's eyes met. Booth attempted to fire the gun again, but nothing happened. As Lincoln went to Rathbone's aide, Booth charged him and stabbed him in the arm. Lincoln fell, and Booth then jumped out of the box and plummeted to the floor below. He injured his leg but was able to scamper across the stage and exit through a side door. On his way out, he stabbed the orchestra leader, William Withers Jr.

In the Presidential box, Mary went to Abe, who was on the floor, bleeding.

"Are you okay?" she asked, checking to see where the blood was coming from.

Abe raised his arm. "He got me in the arm. How's the major?"

Lincoln heard people trying to open the door. He got up and let them in.

"Are you okay, Mr. President?" the first person through the door asked.

"I'll live. We've got to save the major."

Charles Leale, a young Army surgeon, pushed through the crowd to get to Major Rathbone, while another doctor, Charles Sabin Taft, was lifted up to the box from the stage. They went to Clara, who held the major and sobbed. Dr. Leale and Taft checked to see where Rathbone had been stabbed, thinking that was the weapon used.

After Taft and Leale opened Rathbone's shirt, they found no stab wound, but Leale did locate the gunshot wound behind the left ear. The two doctors looked at one another and then at Clara.

"What's wrong?" she asked.

"He's not going to make," Dr. Taft said with sadness in his eyes.

3

Clara let out a piercing scream that was heard throughout Ford's Theatre.

*   *   *

Lincoln Douglas shot up from his bed as his bullhorn-sounding alarm clock came on. He was a handsome, thirty-year-old, brown-skinned black guy with a bald head. After he cleared his eyes, he looked at his digital clock on the wall and saw that the time was 7 AM and the date was June 10, 2025.

"Damn, man, what were you dreaming about? It seemed so real," he said, scratching his head. Then he remembered something. "Shoot, I'm going to be late!" He quickly jumped out of bed and ran into the shower.

About fifteen minutes later, Lincoln was running down the alley like he had been shot out of a canon, jumping over puddles of water whenever he saw them. He wore navy blue sweatpants and a matching hoodie, with a Coach backpack slung over one shoulder. His chiseled physique and handsome looks made him look like a Greek god heading to battle.

As he cut through a few backyards, he came to the main street. He looked up and saw a train leaving the station. He increased his speed as he ran up the stairs of the Purple Line Davis Street Station, near Northwestern University in Evanston, Illinois. When he got to the platform, his train had pulled up, and he darted onto it with a last-minute burst just before the doors closed. Smiling as usual, he approached a young woman from behind and pretended to snatch her bag. She turned around in haste, pulling her bag back.

"Gotcha!" he said.

The young woman rolled her eyes. "Late as usual. You lucky. I was about to use my stun gun. I've been waiting on the opportunity. You would be a good person to try it out on."

"Dang, Sonia, I see you woke up on the wrong side of the bed this morning."

"Sorry, baby," Sonia said as she kissed Lincoln on the mouth. "But you can't keep acting like you're going to rob somebody."

"Just joking around with you."

Sonia snuggled up to him and smiled as they kissed some more. He stared into her hazel brown eyes and melted. She had a supermodel face, but her body was fit and curvy. She was mixed Latino and black, in her late twenties, with long, flowing sandy-brown hair.

"You know you make me weak when you do that," Lincoln said, running his hands up and down her back.

She snickered. "A woman got to use what she got to get what she wants."

"And what exactly is that?"

She looked him dead in his face. "You know what that is, Lincoln."

"Is this how Sonia Douglas going to act in the future?" Lincoln cringed, knowing that he shouldn't have asked that question.

Sonia smiled at him and gently placed her hand on his chest. "Is that a proposal?"

Lincoln stared off into space, thinking of ways to respond to her question.

Sonia grabbed his cheeks with her hand. "Cat got your tongue, Mr. Douglas?"

He smiled. "My tongue is fine. You and I will have our day in the sun eventually."

"When?" she pressed. She really wanted to know the answer.

"I passed the bar," he said, hoping to lighten the mood.

"Me too, idiot." Sonia wasn't in a playing mood about their relationship. "Two years ago."

"See, our day in the sun is sooner than you think." Lincoln smiled at her.

Sonia huffed. "I hope you don't think you're going to have a successful career being late all the time. Right now, you look like you're heading to be the first husband in the White House."

"Does it always have to be a competition with you?" he asked, rolling his eyes.

"Life is about winners and losers. What side do you want to be on in the end? I know I'm going to be very successful. You better recognize. You can't find or buy a better woman than me."

Lincoln brushed off her comments. "Who cares about a successful career? I want to be legendary."

Sonia almost choked as she laughed loudly at him. "Really? Lincoln, you have such an imagination."

"No imagination. I've passed the bar. I was a Secret Service agent at the White House for four years. Hated it, but I did it. I have been a police officer for CPD for the last five years. I'm a damn good cop. Plus, I made captain last month. And I just found out this morning that I'm going to work in the Unsolved Crimes Unit. I might be the next Barry Obama. Are you ready to be Michelle?" he asked with a snicker.

Sonia held out her ring finger.

"Do we have to do this today?" he asked, hoping to avoid the marriage conversation.

"Okay. I'll give you a break today. So, you're serious about going to work with your uncle Terrence?" Sonia slit her eyes at him.

"Yep. It's a done deal."

"I thought you two had issues?"

Lincoln became uncomfortable. "We did, but that's now in the past."

"So, what happened for you to move on? You know, you're a very stubborn person to deal with at times. Not that I know anything about it," she said, rolling her eyes.

"I forgave him. It did hurt that he didn't come to my law school graduation and other things, but I can't hold on to those old feelings forever."

"That's big of you. My baby is growing up," Sonia joked as she put her ring finger back in his face.

"Not really. My uncle is a lonely man. All he got is me. After my parents died, he stepped up and took care of me. He became a super cop, but he forgot that he had a family at times. He wasn't a deadbeat uncle or anything like that. He was just not there when I needed him to be like a father."

"It's in the past now. It had to be tough on the both of you with your parents dying in a car accident."

Lincoln looked at the buildings the train passed by, thinking about what she had just said.

"I know I can't change the past. So, I have to move forward," he said. Suddenly he stopped talking. An image of his uncle grabbing him and running away from people chasing them entered his thoughts. It puzzled him because he didn't remember the moment ever happening in his life.

Sonia saw the blank stare out to nowhere on his face. "Are you okay?"

Lincoln snapped out of it. "Yeah, I just got a lot on my mind."

"If moving forward includes me, then I want to know what's on your mind so that I can help you, Lincoln. You don't have to carry everything by yourself anymore. I'm here for you. I want a future with you. Team Douglas."

Lincoln looked her in the face and then turned his gaze away. Though he had dated Sonia off and on for over four years, he hadn't told her

7

much about his life before they'd gotten together or his relationship with his uncle. He did hate lying to people, but after years of people showing him pity since his parents were deceased, he had decided to exclude certain pieces of his life from anybody who didn't already know the truth. He definitely didn't want people asking how his parents really died. It hurt him deeply that he held the truth from her. Sonia was special, but he hadn't reached that comfort level with her to share his deepest, darkest secrets. In many ways, he hadn't given her his heart or total trust, which had led to Lincoln's love for other women and their attention. His childhood past was the one thing that kept him from reaching that next level with all the women he dated.

"Did you see that game last night? Trae Young could have scored a hundred points if he'd wanted to," Lincoln said, hoping to change the topic of discussion.

"Still being secretive. And you expect us to be a married couple one day."

"Some things, I like to keep in the past. It has nothing to do with us." He grabbed her by the hand.

Sonia turned to him with a confused look on her face. "That's funny. It seems like your friend Casey knows way more than me about you."

Lincoln took a slight step back. "I know you're not jealous of Casey, are you?"

Sonia exhaled. "Kind of am. He's in your inner circle."

"You shouldn't be," Lincoln said, embracing her.

"It just seems like you two got a secret bond and I'm the outsider. I want in, baby."

Lincoln kissed her forehead. "Sonia, I hope you don't want me to pick you over my friend. I love you, but I don't like ultimatums."

"No, no, that's not what I'm saying. That's not me. You know that," she pleaded.

"Casey is my best friend. He has been there for me since my first day in school here in Chicago."

"Is he dating that girl Sydney?" Sonia asked, with one eye on his face to see his reaction.

Lincoln was flabbergasted. He knew what she was alluding to. "Why do you even care?"

"She seems always to be around. She must be interested in him or…you. I don't trust her."

"Man, can we just have a nice day in the city? I'm meeting Uncle Terrence later to discuss what cases we will be working on."

"Why are you avoiding my questions?" Sonia said with a growl.

"Okay. Sydney is just our friend. We have been friends since I joined the force. She's like a guardian over me at times. She knows what's going on before I do most of the time. I trust her with my life."

"So, you don't trust me with your life?"

"It's not a competition."

Sonia looked him in the face. "So, neither you nor Casey have ever slept with her, ever?"

Lincoln was taken aback. He just wanted to move forward and discuss another topic. "I can't speak for Casey. I know I haven't slept with her. I hope you don't think that I did."

"I hope not. She is beneath you."

"What has she ever done to you?"

"Be around too much. She doesn't know how to stay in her lane. She ain't got no other police friends?" Sonia asked with a smirk.

Lincoln's frustration started to boil over. "Damn, I don't know! You can ask her the next time you see her. You still coming tonight?"

Sonia saw the frustration on his face. "Yes. Baby, I'm sorry. I'm an attorney. I question everything, but I don't question that you love me. I just want to be in your heart."

He pulled her closer to him. "You have my heart, but I can't live a life stuck on the witness stand. All it does is push me away."

"I'm sorry. I will try not to do it again. No promises, though." She smiled.

Lincoln laughed. "I know that much about you."

"So, what are you doing at lunch today?" Sonia placed her hand on his arm.

"You already at lunch? The day's just begun."

"I was hoping maybe we could have lunch together."

Lincoln looked at the calendar on his cell phone. He had 12 to 1 PM marked as busy. "Oh, yeah, I have lunch with Casey today."

Sonia rolled her eyes. "I should have known."

"Let it go, please. Right now, he's the only person to remember that it's my birthday."

"Oh, baby, I didn't forget."

"I can't tell if you did or didn't," Lincoln said, jokingly frowning at her.

Sonia reached into her bag and pulled out a note. She handed it to him. "I'll never forget you, Lincoln. No matter what."

Lincoln took the note and read it to himself. "In love. I love you more than I love breathing. Every time you touch me or look into my eyes, it strengthens me to increase my love and desire for you, the true man of my dreams, yes, you. I don't want to spend just a couple of moments in your arms, even though it is a start. I want this to be the love that you and I will fight for, even if we're not fighting. I want you to yearn for my love, as I do yours, so that we never have to part. Let me show you and lead you to the

10

land of promise, where love and happiness are plentiful and the surroundings are just like you, handsome and gentle. I've waited a lifetime for you, and it was definitely worth the wait because our love was built in the heavens and is as pure as ivory snow. We can conquer the world together and crumble by being apart. You're the master of my soul with the key to my heart. You're a special part of my life that I can never do without. I've loved you since the day I met you, and without you, I don't exist. If I had one wish, it would be to spend not only this day, but all of your birthdays together for the rest of our lives. My love is dedicated to you. Love always, Sonia."

When Lincoln finished reading, he was speechless. His eyes teared up with emotion as her words embraced him.

"Are you okay?" she asked, wondering what he was thinking.

Lincoln smiled. "That was deep. That was beautiful. I don't think anybody will be topping this gift here." He displayed the note.

"I got you something, too, but I'll give that to you later tonight." She winked at him.

"This is more than enough. Sonia, I love you, but I'm not perfect. I'm flawed like the next man. I do want to do what's right in life."

"What do you mean, Lincoln?" she asked, confused by his statement.

Lincoln embraced her and kissed her on the forehead again. He avoided looking her in the face. "Nothing. I want to spend the rest of my birthdays with you, too. By the way, I called you last night several times, but you never answered. What did you do?"

"I had a business meeting with some clients downtown. Then when I got home, I went straight to bed." She looked him dead in the eyes and kissed him. "Plus, my phone has been acting funny lately."

"No problem."

"You didn't stop by, did you?" she asked.

"No, I just wanted to see you."

***

Right at 12 PM, Lincoln, dressed in his police uniform, ran up a flight of stairs and toward an office at the end of the hallway. The door's nameplate read, "Sarah McMillan, Therapist." He passed the receptionist and went directly into the inner office. When he opened the door, he saw a slim-figured blonde woman in her mid-forties, standing by the window. She turned to face him. She was cute, with a lightly tanned and glasses sitting on the bridge of her nose.

"You're late, Mr. Douglas," she said, pointing to the clock on the wall.

"I'm sorry, Sarah. I got tied up doing desk work."

"Sit down," Sarah said in a commanding tone.

Lincoln saw the no-nonsense look on her face and sat down without hesitation.

"So, what is on your mind?" she asked as she sat down across from him with her pen and pad.

Lincoln didn't say anything. He just sat there, looking at her.

"Is that how you want to waste your money? I'm here to help you, but I need to know what I'm helping you with first."

Lincoln scratched his right ear. "I don't know where to start."

"The beginning is a good place. You come here every week and don't say much. I was surprised to hear that you wanted this emergency session today."

He gritted his teeth. "That's fair. You're right. I had a crazy dream that Abraham Lincoln didn't die last night. The night before, I dreamed my parents were important people in the country, almost like royalty. Before

12

"Not that great. Lincoln, you are here with me. She's probably not the one for you."

Lincoln smirked. "Are you the one?"

Sarah giggled. "Are you kidding? Definitely not me."

"But regardless of all that, I do need to find out if she is. This will definitely be the last time."

"You sure?" she said with a smile.

"One hundred percent sure. I have to get my life in order. Can't keep doing this."

"If this is that last time, then I'm going to make it the best time." Sarah kissed him and pulled him even closer.

They embraced each other tightly as they made mad love all over her office.

* * *

Later that evening, at the bar of the Drake Hotel, Casey, Sydney, Lincoln, and Sonia were having happy hour drinks, celebrating Lincoln's thirtieth birthday. The bar was crowded and loud. The foursome sat at a booth in the corner. The guys sat across from each other, as did the women, which didn't sit well with Sonia or Sydney, who hated looking at the other's face. And Sonia constantly being flirtatious with Lincoln only irritated Sydney even more. She did her best to ignore Sonia, but she was reaching a boiling point.

Lincoln saw Sydney's face turn red and knew something had to be done. He cared for both women and wanted them to be civil to one another, but after all these years and countless efforts, it just hadn't worked out. In many ways, he was attracted to Sydney and held a special place for her in his heart, but the moment had never been right for them to explore a relationship. She was smart, sexy, and sassy, which he liked. Her soft, dark skin, light brown eyes, and long jet-black hair gave her a look of an Egyptian

15

queen. Originally from Atlanta, Georgia, she came from a long line of police officers, and her now being one completed her lifelong dream. Though she kept it quiet, she had a mad crush on Lincoln that had started the day they'd first met.

"Hey, Sydney, what happened with you and that fireman you were dating?" Lincoln asked, thinking the question would help get Sonia off his back about any romantic possibilities between him and Sydney.

Sydney gave him a weird glare. She didn't want to talk about her business, especially in front of Sonia. "Really? You putting my business out on Front Street?"

"I'd like to know," Sonia said, chiming in.

Sydney rolled her eyes at Sonia. "I bet you would."

"Okay, now, we're not here to fight. Stop it for one night, ladies, and let's just celebrate my best friends' birthday. Once again, happy thirtieth birthday. Love you, man," Casey said, toasting with Lincoln. Casey was Lincoln's oldest and closest friend. They had met in kindergarten and hadn't separated since. Even though Casey was white, he was colorblind when it came to their relationship.

Lincoln smirked. "Love you, too."

"I still can't believe you are going to work for your uncle," Casey said, shaking his head. "You got so many other opportunities out there. You're the smartest friend I got. If this was a different world, you would be president."

Lincoln rolled his eyes. "Don't need the world going through my garbage, looking for secrets."

"What are you trying to hide?" Sydney asked with a smile and wink.

Sonia hugged his arm and stared at him. "I keep telling him that he is selling himself short. The sky's the limit, Lincoln. I would love to be first lady."

16

"Already first bitch," Sydney said to herself.

"Thanks for all the compliments, but as you all know, I am black in America. And I'm not exactly Obama. I'm a little bit darker." Lincoln laughed.

"I think it's admirable that he's following his dreams. I would fully support that if I were you," Sydney said, slitting her eyes at Sonia.

"I bet you would, but you can't even hold on to a relationship long enough to support it."

"You're right. I just see through the pretentious bullshit that people have and move on before it affects my lifestyle. I'm just smarter than most. What are you on now, four years?" Sydney grinned at Sonia.

"Hey, don't put me in the middle," Lincoln said, hoping to stop the two women's jawing back and forth.

They ignored him.

Sonia looked at Sydney. "I got my relationship in check. What about you? Oops, you don't have one."

"So, when is the big day?" Sydney asked Sonia and Lincoln. Lincoln gave her an evil stare.

Sonia turned to Lincoln. "That question is for you." She then turned back to Sydney. "I guess there's still hope for us being friends." She laughed.

Lincoln sat there, looking at Casey and Sydney with embarrassment. He didn't know how to respond and not cause an argument with Sonia.

"Cat got your tongue?" Sonia asked.

Lincoln felt compelled to respond. "Me and Sonia got some things we need to finish before that next step. I love her, and the plan is to set that date...one day." He saw her death stare and then added, "Soon."

Sonia kissed him on the cheek. "That was nice, baby, but I still don't know what those things are we need to finish."

"Okay, one more round of drinks, and then I need to go see my uncle," Lincoln said, hoping to move on from the relationship talk.

"I have to go to the ladies' room. I'll be right back," Sonia said, getting up and walking away.

"She hates me," Sydney said with a snicker.

"I wouldn't say hate. A strong dislike on the hate meter, definitely," Lincoln said, and they all laughed out loud.

"Sydney, you don't like her, either," Casey said, bursting her bubble.

"We're talking about her, not me. I just hope she's different when I'm not around."

"That goes without saying. I think she thinks it's weird that you hang with us and nobody has slept with you," Lincoln said with a smirk.

Sydney looked at both of them. "Can't be me. I'm smoking hot. Maybe you two give off the gay vibe to me. I feel nothing but a sister-and-brother relationship with the both of you."

"Really, I thought you were playing both sides of the field," Casey said, high-fiving Lincoln.

"You couldn't handle this, anyway. I would break the both of you in half," she said, looking across at Lincoln.

"I'm staying out of the breaking-in-half conversation," he said while trying to get the waiter's attention. He looked down at his watch.

"Tell your old uncle Terrence I said hi," Casey said.

"Before Sonia comes back, I have to tell you guys about the DNA test I took."

Sydney and Casey perked up.

"Why did you take a DNA test?" Casey asked.

"What did you find out?" Sydney asked with great anticipation.

Chapter TWO

At home in his three-bedroom house in Hyde Park, Uncle Terrence sat in front of his TV in the basement, staring into space. His face showed grief. Though an avid TV fan, he hadn't turned it on yet, and judging from his expression, it might not get turned on anytime soon. When he stopped looking into space, his gaze returned to the pamphlet on his lap. Tears filled his eyes as he picked it up and began reading it.

"The impact of Alzheimer's and dementia. Currently, an estimated fifty million people worldwide are living with dementia, including five million Americans." He stopped reading and rubbed his forehead. "Why me?" he said, looking at the ceiling. "You not going to take me without a fight."

He got up and hurried over to his shelves and started rustling through several boxes. It was obvious that he was looking for something very important. He got frustrated whenever what he was looking for was not in the box that he had pulled down from the shelf. After ten boxes, he finally found what he was looking for.

"Dang, T," he said. "You got to stop hiding things from yourself. Your mind isn't as good as it used to be." He laughed. "This is the last thing I need to do."

He combed through different files in the box until he found what he was looking for. Written on the outside of the file were the words "For Lincoln." He grabbed it and tossed the box to the side. Then he made his way over to the La-Z-Boy chair in front of the TV and plopped down. When he opened the file, the first thing he saw was a picture of him carrying a black woman to an ambulance.

"Who are you?" he asked, staring at the picture. "No identity at all. No record of your existence or the people you were with. It just doesn't make any sense. And who wanted you all dead? No witnesses?"

He grabbed several other pictures and stared at them. The pictures were of a shootout at O'Hare Airport. Most of the pictures showed the dead bodies of black people.

"Son of a bitch. I know you were out there laughing at us. God, just give me one clue. I will do the rest of the work. What happened to Lincoln's parents that day?" He picked up pieces of paper from his past investigation and reread them. "It was like they disappeared into thin air and just left him behind. Why was someone trying to kill them?"

Terrence heard someone upstairs, creeping around. He grabbed his gun and slowly made his way over to the basement door. There, he heard a few more footsteps. He braced himself and came up the basement steps, fully charged and ready to shoot. He saw his front door opening up and ran to the opposite side of it. His gun was cocked and ready. As the person came inside and closed the door, Terrence instantly put his gun to the person's head.

"Don't move!"

The person put their hands in the air. "Unc, it's me, Lincoln! Is this my birthday surprise?"

"Happy birthday!" Terrence put his gun to his side and looked at Lincoln. "Didn't you come in the house already? I thought I heard someone up here."

Lincoln stared at his uncle with a concerned look on his face. "I just got here." He turned on some lights and walked around the house. "Looks safe to me."

"I could have sworn someone was up here."

Lincoln hugged his uncle. Terrence was shocked by the affection. "Unc, maybe you're working too many hours."

Terrence smiled. "Don't get mad because I'm outworking you."

"I'm not sure that's a healthy competition," Lincoln said, looking at his uncle with concern.

"I wish I could have been a better uncle to you," Terrence said, staring at Lincoln's face. "After your mother and father died, I didn't know anything to offer you besides safety."

Lincoln smiled. "I definitely grew up safe."

Terrence exhaled. "Hey, take a seat, and I'll go grab the files."

"Okay, but I can come downstairs."

Terrence put his hands up, stopping that notion from happening. "No, I will bring the files up."

He rushed down the stairs, threw the pamphlet about dementia under the La-Z-Boy seat cushion, grabbed the case files, and returned back upstairs. Lincoln was standing near the fireplace, looking at old family pictures, when Terrence reentered the room.

"So, what deadly secrets are you hiding down there?" Lincoln said with a chuckle.

Terrence tightened his lips as he sat down on the sofa. "Son, I want you to know that I am so excited that you will be joining my division."

"No, they are not. I found them years ago. I didn't contact them, but checked them out and there is no connection between them where they were ever in the same state."

"Then how come nothing has ever happened in the past?" Lincoln asked slitting his eyes at his uncle.

"I made up your records. I created a birth certificate and adoption papers. That's why your birth certificate says you were born in Canada. Believe me, someone is coming after you. I know it."

Lincoln burst out with laughter at his uncle. "Now I know you are tripping. I'm not running anywhere. It's just a DNA test."

"You see all the dead people in those pictures? None of them had any record or DNA in our system. They were like ghosts."

"That doesn't mean anything. You are overreacting." Lincoln looked at the pictures again.

"Lincoln, we need to go asap. I got enough money stored away for us to disappear."

"Man, Uncle Terrence, you must be going through some tough times. It just sounds like my parents left me and didn't come back for me. And now they don't want to own up to having me as a child. It hurts. You and I are good. I'm upset that you didn't tell me years ago, but at least you never left me."

Terrence saw that Lincoln wasn't leaving Chicago based on what he'd just told him. "Okay, but if something happens, promise me you will leave and disappear forever. I can live with me dying, but not you."

"Unc, I'm good. So, I'm gonna pass on working that case with you. I'm sure there are a million other cases that I can jump on next week when I join your team."

Terrence mustered up a fake grin. "Sure. Let's grab lunch tomorrow to celebrate your birthday?"

Lincoln smiled. "Definitely, I'll drop by your division at 12 PM tomorrow."

"Make it Navy Pier. Meet at the entrance."

"You gonna be alright?" Lincoln asked, seeing the concern still on Terrence's face.

"I'm sure everything will be alright," Terrence said, trying to make Lincoln feel safe about things.

Lincoln checked his watch. "I got to go. I have to meet Sonia at 10 PM tonight at the Comedy Club."

Terrence nervously laughed. "She seems like a good woman. Sydney is even better."

Lincoln tilted his head as he looked at his uncle. "You sure you haven't been drinking?"

"Nope."

Terrence remembered something before Lincoln walked out the door. "Hold up."

"What now, Unc?"

Terrence ran over to the fireplace, reached up the chimney, and grabbed a small notepad.

"Take this." He handed the notepad to Lincoln.

"What's this for?" Lincoln asked, clueless.

"These are all the accounts I have. Altogether, it's about five million dollars. Just read the instructions on what to do and who to contact."

"Damn!" Lincoln smiled. "That's a lot."

"Listen, if something happens, I want you to take the money and leave."

Lincoln saw the seriousness in his uncle's eyes. "Okay. I got it. See you tomorrow at lunch. Get some sleep tonight, okay?"

As Lincoln eased out the door, he and his uncle locked eyes.

"So, he left over an hour ago?"

"Yeah. I just got back from the Southside when he was leaving. Are you the person he was meeting?"

"Yeah, kind of, I think, but not at eleven."

Sydney smirked. "Were you late again?"

"Not today, Syd."

"What were you meeting about?"

"Nothing big, just my birthday lunch. We do it every year."

"I still need to give you my gift. Didn't want to give it to you last night. Don't want to come between you and Miss Thang." Sydney smiled.

Lincoln smiled. "You don't have to give me anything. You are like an angel to me."

"It's nothing much. Just showing you, I care."

His conversation with his uncle came to mind. "Was my uncle acting strange?"

"A little, but he always gets that pep in his step when things are going his way. He seemed to be alright."

"And he left alone?"

"Yeah, why?"

"Just wondering where he could be. It's almost 12:30 now. He didn't even answer my calls."

"That's definitely not his style, to let things slide," Sydney said, now concerned as well. "I'll ask around, see if maybe something came up. What are you going to do?"

Lincoln checked his watch again. "I'm going to go to his house and see if maybe he went home."

"I'll meet you there."

"Okay, bye," Lincoln said, and then he hung up and drove off.

***

When Lincoln got to his uncle's house, he saw Terrence's car parked in the driveway. It was totally out of character for Terrance to just blow off a meeting, especially with Lincoln.

Lincoln's suspicions increased. He pulled out his service revolver and slowly walked around the house, looking through the windows. He saw nothing out of the ordinary and heard nothing. The second was what bothered him. He knew that if Terrence was inside, the TV would be on, or there would be some type of movement inside. He used his house key and opened the door. Then he slowly peeked inside and walked in.

He crept around the first floor of the house but found nothing out of the ordinary. He saw the basement door was open, and he went over and down. When he got to the basement, he saw that it looked like a tornado had hit it. He walked over to the couch to see if someone was behind it. Looking down, he noticed the pamphlet about dementia lying on the floor.

"Shit!" he said to himself sad. "That explains a lot." He put the pamphlet in his back pocket and continued his search, but he didn't find his uncle in the basement.

Lincoln crept back up the stairs, toward Terrence's bedroom on the second floor, a little nervous and very scared. He feared the worst thing imaginable: that his uncle might be dead. He opened the bedroom door and immediately became ill. There was so much blood around the room and on the bed. As he got closer, he saw a naked woman and his uncle lying there, seemingly dead. Lincoln turned away from the sight.

Things quickly changed when he heard Terrence cough. Lincoln then checked his uncle's pulse, and the woman's, too. Terrence had a weak pulse, but the woman was dead. Lincoln checked to see where his uncle had been shot, and he discovered that he had been hit in the left shoulder and the they just don't want you messing with their money." Casey gave her a nudge and wink.

"So, Lincoln is money?"

Casey nodded. He pointed over at Lincoln and Sonia, who were still hugged up. "Money and investor together."

"Yeah, that combination doesn't last long. Love has to be free. No pressure." Sydney smiled at him.

"What do you know about love?"

"I know that's not love."

Casey stared at her.

"What are you staring at?" Sydney asked.

"You."

"What about me?"

"I knew it since day one, but you finally confirmed it."

Sydney gave him a weird glare. "Confirmed what?"

"You got the hots for Lincoln."

"No, I don't."

"Okay, all I'm saying is that if do, you better speak up soon. You never know what might happen. Living with regret is hard to do."

"Even if I did feel a certain way about him, he's with her over there," Sydney said, rolling her eyes at Sonia.

"Sometimes, you have to gamble on love. I get rejected all the time."

Sydney laughed. "You got no game."

"Better to play the game than sit on the bench, watching," Casey said, nudging her on the arm.

A slew of officers came into the waiting area. Behind them came the chief of police, Monty Clayborn, and Walter Smith, Terrence's old partner. Both men were over fifty, white-haired and thick around the waist. The only difference in their appearance, besides their clothes, was that Walter had a bushy mustache. Monty noticed Sonia and Lincoln hugging and went over to them.

"Lincoln," he said forcefully. The room got extremely quiet.

Lincoln rose up and looked at him. "Yes, Chief Clayborn. Hey, Uncle Walt."

"You doing alright, Lincoln?" Walter asked.

"I'm dealing with it, Uncle Walt."

"What's the status, son?" Monty asked.

Lincoln looked around at the eyes in the room staring at him, and then he turned his attention back to the chief. "He was shot twice, once in the shoulder and the other in the abdomen. He's been in surgery now for over two hours. Besides that, I don't know."

Monty glared at Sonia. He wanted her to remove herself from the seat next to Lincoln so that they could talk, but she could care less about what he wanted. Working in the prosecutor's office, Sonia felt that she was just as important as the chief, and she wasn't going to budge an inch. Seeing her resistance, Monty decided to go another route.

"Let's talk over there," he said to Lincoln, walking to the window. Though the room was now crowded, the officers standing by the window scattered off once they saw their chief coming that way. Lincoln followed him.

"So, did you know about this affair your uncle was having with this unknown woman? Who is she?"

Lincoln stared Monty dead in the eyes. "No. I didn't find out that this woman existed until today. And I still don't know who she is."

"It just seems odd that he kept this secret from all of us. This woman doesn't exist in any of our systems. It's not like Terrence to break immigration laws by harboring an illegal."

"I don't see no other person standing out here, so yes, I'm threatening you."

Walter saw the fire in Monty's eyes. He knew he was not joking around. "This is not my fault," he said, hoping to defuse the situation.

"Then why is Terrence lying in the hospital? Still alive, I remind you. Lincoln should have been delivered to our friends. Don't you know how to follow orders correctly!"

"You can't blame him still living on me."

"Then who should I blame…him?" Monty stared at Walter like he wanted to punch a hole through him. "This is not good."

"Why?" Walter asked. "And what is this all about, anyway? They are like family to me, and to you, too."

"I don't know, and I don't care. At the end of the day, these are just two niggers living in our city. Some government agency wants this done, and they are paying us a lot to make sure it gets done. Are you having second thoughts?"

"I'll fix it. I promise," Walter begrudgingly replied.

Monty chuckled. "I know you will." He walked off to his car, and Walter did the same.

When Walter got in the car, he took out his phone to make a call. "Hey, I need you right now. No excuses. Meet me at the old warehouse in fifteen minutes. You didn't do the job."

"Jimmy is dead!" Sergio said angrily.

"And you failed to get the guy and kill his uncle."

Sergio was surprised. "He's still alive?"

"Yeah. Did he see you?"

Sergio paused before responding. "No."

"Well, the job is still not done." Walter hung up the phone.

46

***

Sergio looked over at Tommy, who was packing his suitcase. "Hold off on the leaving right now. We got more work to do. That nigger didn't die."

Tommy huffed. "This is a bad idea."

"Unless you want to be looking over your shoulder for the rest of your life, wondering if that person in the supermarket is there to kill you, then you best get on board and help me finish the job."

"I'm in," Tommy said, throwing the suitcase back into the hotel closet. "What about the other one?"

"We got to get him, too. He should be easy. I'm sure he'll be lurking around the hospital, checking on his uncle. I'm calling Raul. We need a third guy." Sergio pulled out his gun and checked the clip.

Chapter THREE

About an hour later, outside of Tammy's Bar and Grill, Lincoln walked back to his car with Sonia. Judging from her folded-up arms, she was definitely mad about something. She noticed that he had gotten several text messages from his doctor. She'd caught that much by quickly glancing down at his phone. She kept her eyes on his phone light as it blinked, alerting him to another text. Sonia thought that was suspicious, especially when it blinked five times in a row. Lincoln saw her looking and tried to cut off his alert settings, but it was too late.

"Who is that?" Sonia asked with attitude as she stood by the car door, waiting for him to open it.

"Damn, why do you care? It's my phone."

Lincoln put his phone in his back pocket and opened up the car door for her. He went to his side of the car and got in. He wanted to text Sarah back so that she would stop the onslaught of text messages, but he couldn't. With so many things running through his mind, the last thing he wanted was to discuss how he had been sleeping with Mayor McMillan's wife, his therapist, for over a year. He knew Sarah had been texting him to find out

back of the head. When the officer slumped to the ground, Raul noticed that the man was a mannequin. He then raced into the room, unsure what to do next. He stopped in his tracks when he saw no one in the bed. He quickly turned to escape the room but ran right into Lincoln and more Chicago PD officers with their guns cocked and ready to fire.

"Drop the gun," Lincoln demanded, hoping to avoid a shootout.

Raul wouldn't comply. He raised his gun, but Lincoln and another officer fired twice, laying him out on the hospital floor.

From down the hallway, Sonia raced over to Lincoln. "Who is he?"

Lincoln shrugged. "I have no idea."

She peeked inside the room. "Where is your uncle?" she asked, turning on the lights.

Lincoln walked over to his bed. "Somewhere safe for now."

As they headed to the elevator door, Lincoln got a call from Sydney. Unlike the calls from Sarah, he knew he had to answer.

"What's up? Is everything okay with my uncle?" he asked.

"I need you to come to the garage now. There's a problem," she said, sounding distressed.

"What is it?"

"Come now, Lincoln," she said and then hung up.

"Who was that?" Sonia asked. She saw the tension on his face.

"Sydney."

"What drama now?"

"She's in the basement with my uncle. Something isn't right. I want you to get off on the first floor. Go home, and if you don't hear from me in thirty minutes, contact Walter and Monty."

Lincoln pushed the elevator button hard. When it came, he jumped on it, paranoid about what was waiting for him in the garage. He pushed the first-floor button and the basement button. When the elevator got to the first floor, he made Sonia get off. She didn't want to, but he didn't take no for an answer. He knew that whatever was down in the basement; she wasn't able to protect him from it.

When the elevator reached the basement, it was dark and quiet. Over on the other end of the garage sat a white van. He saw hands waving him over and heard Sydney's voice. He ran over to them. Looking in the van, he saw Sydney and three black people, two men and one woman, whom he had never before seen in his life. One of the men and the woman were dressed in hospital scrubs while they attended to Terrence.

"What's going on here?" Lincoln asked, trying to figure things out.

"I'm Doctor Simpson," the lady in the van said as she checked Terrence's vitals.

"What's going on, Sydney?" Lincoln asked again.

"I don't exactly know where to begin, but these people say that they can protect us and save your uncle, but you need to come with them."

"I'm not going nowhere with you people. I don't know you," Lincoln said, raising his voice. "Get my uncle out of here."

The black man on the opposite side of Terrence looked at Lincoln. "If you do not come, your uncle will die. Is that what you want? We are not here to harm you. That's a promise."

"Where are we going?" Sydney asked.

"She doesn't need to go," the man driving the van said.

"If I go, she goes. That's the only way this is happening." Lincoln looked at his uncle. "Let's get this over with."

Lincoln jumped in the van, and they drove off. Thirty minutes later, they arrived at a private abandoned airplane hangar. Still nervous about the situation, Lincoln and Sydney pulled out their guns.

"You can kill us, and your uncle will die with us," Doctor Simpson said without any emotion. "This is the only way we save you and your uncle."

"Just tell me where we are going?" Lincoln pleaded. "And why do you need me?"

"Your honor, I'm Peter, chief minister of peace. We are just going to take your uncle to a hospital in our home country and take you to meet your family. They are waiting on you, especially with what is now transpiring. The DNA test you took alerted not only us, but also your government. They killed one of us. Our secretary of defense was the woman found in bed with him."

"Your honor?" Sydney asked. "Home country?"

Lincoln ignored her questions for his own. "Why is my DNA test so important?"

"Let's just get on the flight. Your family will tell you everything. You have my sworn promise."

"What family are you talking about?" Lincoln asked. "He's the only family I got."

"Not true. They will tell you everything when you meet them."

"Let's go," Lincoln said, knowing he had to save his uncle's life more than anything else. He was also very intrigued by the prospect of meeting his family.

They all got out of the van and boarded the plane.

Lincoln turned to Sydney. "You don't have to go."

"Ride or die. Plus, I'm off this weekend. Free trip. And I want to make sure you and Terrence are okay."

Lincoln's phone vibrated. He looked down and saw that it was Sonia. "Damn," he said. He texted her that he would contact her in twenty minutes. She texted back an angry emoji face.

He and Sydney buckled up.

"I'm nervous," Sydney said, staring into his eyes.

"Shit, I'm scared. This is like a movie or something. Last night, my uncle told me some stuff that I didn't believe. And then, when I saw that he might have dementia, I just thought it was crazy talk, but now things don't seem so crazy after all."

Sydney looked at Lincoln like he was crazy. "Don't you think that is some information that you might have shared with me before I agreed to jump on this plane to who knows where?"

"Oops. My bad," he said, grabbing her hand.

Doctor Simpson came back to them. "Once we arrive, things will become clearer to you; that, I promise." She buckled up, and the plane jetted off like Terrence had told him it had the day he'd found Lincoln.

***

About ten minutes after the plane took off, Walter, Monty, and two of the hired hands, that Walter was using, Sergio and Tommy, arrived at the private hangar. As the men discussed what had happened, three black Cadillac SUVs pulled up. Two business-dressed white men, one tall and the other short, with six guys dressed like Special Tactical Forces, got out of the SUVs. Monty, being the police chief, decided to take the lead for his group of men.

"Finally, we meet," Monty said, approaching the two businessmen. The six special forces men spread out to secure the perimeter of the hangar.

"Where are they?" the taller man asked with a raised voice. "You told me that you had it all taken care of!"

"Calm down," Monty said, looking at how the special forces had spread out. "This is not our fault. They got Sydney involved, and she helped them escape. The girlfriend, Sonia, is still in play. We got her."

Chapter FOUR

The flight took about two hours. There was a little turbulence as it came through what looked like a hole in the sky. It landed at a private hangar in Douglasville, Florida. Upon arrival, paramedics rushed onto the plane, escorted uncle Terrence off and into an ambulance, and drove him from the airport.

When Lincoln and Sydney exited the plane, they noticed what looked like a small parade outside. They saw the signs and happy faces as they walked down the steps to the tarmac. Sydney glanced at Lincoln, trying to figure out what the place was and what Lincoln had to do with it. When they got to the bottom of the steps, they were both greeted by several people. As they got to the end of the line of well-wishers, a man dressed in a white suit, with a hat to match, approached them. About thirty feet away waited several black SUV limousines.

"Hi, I'm David. I'm your executive administrator. Please walk with me." He led them to the SUV limousines. "I will educate you on what your responsibilities are, who to trust, and anything else that comes up. You will be staying at the king's castle. There are several mansions on the grounds, but yours is right next to the castle. Tonight, you will be staying in the castle with the king and queen."

"So, the king is my father?" Lincoln asked, a puzzled look on his face.

"King of what? Rap?" Sydney asked, looking around at the surroundings, trying to gauge what was really happening. "We better not be going to Jay-Z's house."

"King of Sea Islands," David said, thinking they had been informed. But when he looked over at Dr. Simpson and she shook her head, indicating that they hadn't had that discussion, David realized that this was going to be a challenge. "Okay, when we get to the castle, the king and queen will tell you all about Sea Islands."

"So, the king and queen are my mother and father?" Lincoln was still confused by everything that was being said.

"And Sea Islands is a country? Sydney asked.

David stopped for a moment to answer them. "Yes. Sea Islands is a great nation. We are very wealthy here."

"We didn't travel that far," she said with a smirk. "And when did this Sea Islands become a nation?"

"Eighteen ninety-eight, to be exact. That's when we achieved our independence. Right after the Spanish-American War."

Lincoln looked up and saw a "Welcome to Douglasville" sign. He leaned over to Sydney. "This doesn't seem right," he whispered in her ear.

Sydney looked back at the plane. "Too late now to make a run for it."

"So, what country are we in now?" Lincoln asked.

58

"This is Sea Islands. The state is Florida, and the city is Douglasville. Named after your family," David said, looking over at Lincoln.

"But you just said the state is Florida. Florida is in the United States," Lincoln said, still confused.

"Not here. Not in this universe." David was becoming frustrated.

"I have never heard of a Douglasville in Florida," said Sydney.

David sensed that they were not at ease with their new surroundings, nor did they understand that they were now in a different universe. "Just relax. Your parents have waited a lifetime to see you again. Our entire nation never thought you would return."

"Are they expecting me to stay?" Lincoln asked. "I got a life back in Chicago."

They walked up to the last black SUV. The driver held the door for them to get in. Lincoln and Sydney did not get in. They wanted to finish their questions first.

"You're the heir to the throne," David said with a smile. "This your home. Why would you want to leave?"

"A king? Really? This has got to be a joke." Sydney rolled her eyes. "This ain't America's Florida. You guys just have the same name."

"This is Sea Islands, not the United States," David snapped. "I'm sorry, sir. My behavior is unbecoming. I deeply apologize."

"No problem. So, I don't have any siblings?" Lincoln asked.

"You have two sisters, but you're the first-born male, and only males can rule our nation."

"Have you ever heard of equality?" Sydney said, irked by David's comment.

David ignored her response. "Let's go, and you will see that life here is beautiful." He signaled for the driver to get in the car. Then he held the

59

door open and insisted that they get in. "If you don't like it here, I will personally take you back to Chicago."

"Cool, that's all I'm saying. This might be cool for you, but Chicago is my town. I just want my uncle better. I'll meet my parents, but that's about it. They left me, and I have no problem in leaving them."

"That's fine, sir."

Lincoln and Sydney finally got in the car.

Lincoln looked around the SUV. "I must say this, David. I do like the way you guys roll over here."

"Thank you, sir," David replied as he tapped on the separator window for the driver to take off.

***

Back in Chicago, Sonia was at home, pissed that she hadn't heard back from Lincoln. She had repeatedly called his number, and every time, it had gone directly to voicemail. Feeling desperate, she called Sydney's number several times, but it did the same thing. Even though she knew that his uncle's life was on the line, the last thing she wanted was for Lincoln to be consoled in Sydney's arms, or worse than that, in her bed.

She made herself a drink and then sat down in front of the TV. She was about to call Walter, but then she saw that the news was doing a story about two police deaths. She turned it up. The reporter said that there two police officers had been gunned down right along with two police informants. When she heard that the two officers were Monty and Walter, she knew that Lincoln was somehow involved.

"What the hell is going on?" she asked herself as she tried calling Lincoln again. This time, when he didn't answer, she tossed the phone across the room. "You know I hate being left in the dark! Where are you, Lincoln?"

"My wife," Lincoln said, hoping to press down on the brakes to stop Dalilah's advances.

Sydney was shocked by his response. "Your wife?"

"Yes, my lovely wife," Lincoln said, giving her a look that said he needed her to help him. "Sydney is her name."

"Only one?" Dalilah asked.

"Yeah, only one," Lincoln replied.

Dalilah smiled. "In the Sea Islands and Kenya, it's legal for a man to have two women as wives."

"Douglasville? You should call this place Playersville," Sydney said, laughing.

"Where are the king and queen?" Lincoln asked Dalilah.

"They are coming downstairs now."

"Lincoln, is that you?" said Ayanna, Lincoln's mother, as she gazed at him from the doorway. She was in tears.

The room became silent as everyone awaited his response. Lincoln looked at his mother and father in the doorway, his emotions filled with both anger and joy.

"I'm Lincoln, and this is Sydney," he said, frozen in place. "My wife."

Ayanna ran to him and hugged him with all her heart. She touched him like she didn't really believe he was actually there in the flesh.

"I have missed you and never stopped loving you, my baby boy. You have grown to be such a handsome man."

His father, Jasani, slowly approached. He studied Lincoln's face and body as if he didn't think he was actually the real Lincoln.

Lincoln saw his strange look. "Is there something wrong?"

"How do I know you're actually our son? Many impersonators have come through here."

Lincoln looked at Sydney and then back at his father. "You brought me here. I have no problem going back to Chicago, where you left me the first time. I just need to know how my uncle is doing."

Ayanna saw that things were falling apart. "Jasani, stop. This is our son. Look at his hands," she demanded.

Everyone looked at Lincoln's hands, even him. Jasani saw the birthmark, and tears raced down his face. He walked over to Lincoln and hugged him.

"Son, I am so sorry. It was all my fault. Don't blame the lost years on your mother, Ayanna."

Lincoln didn't know what to say.

"So, what happened?" Sydney asked.

"And you are?" Jasani asked her.

"That's his wife," Dalilah answered, agitated.

"Hi, I'm King Jasani, and this is my wife, Queen Ayanna. I'm sorry for meeting you this way."

"Let's sit down and talk," Ayanna said, leading the way to the large circular sofa in front of the TV. They all sat down.

Jasani noticed that Dalilah was sitting down, too. "Dalilah, please give us some privacy. We want to talk to our son alone." He motioned for the guards at the door to open it for her to leave.

Dalilah got up and walked out of the room.

"Is everyone comfortable?" Ayanna asked.

"I just want to know what happened," Lincoln said, looking at Ayanna and Jasani.

Jasani nodded. "It was twenty-five years ago. We traveled to your world and had a meeting with your government. We thought bridging the gap between the two universes would help both of us understand how to survive, but they didn't want peace. They only wanted to take by any means necessary."

"So, you just left me?" Lincoln asked.

"No," Ayanna said. "You were with your nanny. You supposedly walked away from her. When the white men started shooting at us, we escaped, thinking you and her were on the plane, waiting. When we got back on the plane, we took off. We came back to get you, but we couldn't find you anywhere. We figured that they had killed you, but when you took that DNA test, it triggered an alert for your government and for us. They want to use you to get to us. We're an advanced universe."

"What makes you more advanced than us?" Sydney asked with an attitude. "No one is more advanced than the United States of America. Our country is a superpower."

"We listen to people and share knowledge. In your world, the black person is deemed ignorant unless he has money. And the ones who have money only care about their own growth. I don't see many of your black people combining their wealth together to build empires," Jasani said, coming right back at Sydney with the same attitude.

"Hold on, are we just going to skip over the 'bridging the gap between two universes' statement?" Sydney asked, looking at everyone sitting there. "Call me crazy, but there is only one universe."

"Sydney, right?" Jasani asked.

Sydney nodded.

"In your world, President Lincoln died in 1865 at the hands of John Wilkes Booth. In our universe, Lincoln lived until he died of natural causes in 1901. In your world, he's celebrated as the greatest president ever. In this world, he's ranked as the worst president ever."

65

"I don't believe you," Sydney said, getting up from the sofa. She pulled her phone out and tried to use it, but it didn't work. "Can I use a phone, please?"

Ayanna handed her phone to her. Sydney looked at it for several minutes, trying to figure it out. "How do I get to Google?"

"What's Google?" Ayanna asked.

"How did this happen?"

Jasani stared at her and Lincoln. "In our world, President Lincoln didn't die. He never reversed Special Field Order Number Fifteen, which promised freemen and former slaves plots of land no larger than forty acres. And with Lincoln's separatist mindset, all of the governments that the US collected through wars were given to us black people to manage and run. The white men in America didn't have time to deal with Puerto Rico, Cuba, the Virgin Islands, or any other place where the people were considered native and stupid. We built our nation up slowly and took over South Carolina, Florida, Georgia, Alabama, and Mississippi. Unlike in your world, black people are not dependent on handouts from the government. Our unity is strong. Our unity is prosperous. It's not about individualism here. We want everyone to be their best person."

"I can't believe America would allow this Black States of America to exist." Sydney still wasn't convinced. She sat down again and stared over at Ayanna. "You seem like a person who tells the truth. Do you know Bill Gates?"

"Yes, he's one of the richest people in the world," Ayanna said, glancing over at Jasani, who smiled back at her.

"What about Oprah Winfrey?"

"We have heard of her in your world, but in our world, she never became successful."

"You know Jay-Z?"

66

"Is his wife going to be a problem in making sure he stays? I talked to my father, and he says that this union has to happen for our nations to work together in the future."

"Lincoln will come around," Jasani said, feeling the pressure from Dalilah's words.

"I'm not losing my son twice," Ayanna said, and then she got up and walked out of the room.

Jasani looked over at Dalilah. He thought she would have left with his wife. "Dalilah, tell your father and mother I said hello. Have a good night," he said politely, kicking her out the room and house.

After she left, he looked at the picture of him, his father, and a young Lincoln. "I have to keep my family together even if it means war between the Americans and us."

Chapter FIVE

As Sonia fell asleep in front of her TV, she was woken up by knocks on her door. Startled, she fumbled to turn the volume on the TV down a bit. She slowly moved to the door and looked out the peephole. It stunned her when she saw what seemed like ten to fifteen police officers with their guns drawn like they were ready to shoot when the door opened.

"Who is it?" she yelled as she went into her closet and put on her tennis shoes and a jacket. She figured that when they came inside, they would be taking her down to the station for whatever reason. She grabbed her cell phone and checked to see if she'd gotten another message from Lincoln.

"Damn you," she said when she saw that he'd never texted her back. She walked back over to the door.

"It's Captain Johnson from CPD. Please open up."

Captain Johnson motioned for some of his officers to go around back, thinking Sonia and whoever was inside might try to make a run for it.

"One minute," she said, looking through the peephole again. She then texted Lincoln: "I hope you are happy, but I'm about to be questioned about your shit. Where are you?"

"If you don't open up the door, I'll have someone knock it down!" the captain yelled.

Sonia put her phone in her jacket pocket and opened the door.

"Damn, what could you want with me with at this hour of the night?" she asked, rolling her eyes at the captain.

"We're looking for Lincoln Douglas," the captain said, staring into her house from the doorway.

"He doesn't live here."

The captain shoved a piece of paper in her face. "I already got the warrant."

"Well, he's still not here," she said, moving to the side so that the officers could come in. "Go check. But please don't make a mess of my place. I do work for the DA."

Several of the officers entered her place. They combed through every room but found nothing.

"I know you don't think Lincoln had something to do with what happened tonight to the chief of police?"

"Ms. Richmond, if you know anything, it's best that you tell me now. There are a lot of angry police officers in these streets. I wouldn't want something bad happening to Lincoln."

"So, you think that the person who did this is the black officer? Damn, you racist against your own. I guess it's dark blue versus light blue on the police force."

"You want this to be the hard way for Lincoln?"

"What are you talking about? You know Lincoln wouldn't kill the chief, and definitely not Walter."

"No one is saying he would, but when you disappear right when people are being murdered, it's kind of a red flag. Can't even find his uncle. And he was shot a couple of times. Maybe you don't know Lincoln as well as you think. Some people snap and do things no one ever imagined they would. Since his uncle is not in any hospital in Chicago, there's a good chance he's dead, too. He can't survive without medical care."

"If Lincoln was white, would you have these same thoughts?"

The captain's face turned red. "Don't make this a race thing."

"Sometimes the facts uncover true feelings."

The captain looked over at another officer. "Arrest her for withholding evidence in a criminal investigation."

"What am I withholding?" Sonia shouted as the officer came over, read her her rights, and then handcuffed her.

"See you downtown." The captain smiled as she was ushered away to a patrol car. "Where could this jackass be?" he said to himself.

As he turned to walk out, he noticed that Sonia had been taken out of the patrol car and was being escorted to another vehicle, one with government plates on it. He rushed over.

"She's a potential witness in a murder investigation," he said to the agent, who closed the door to the car that he'd just put Sonia in.

The agent, a white male with rough features and a mean mug, dressed in black, looked at the captain like he was nobody. "This is a matter of national security." He went to the driver's side and opened his door.

The captain grabbed the door before the agent could close it. "Someone murdered the chief of police. I need her testimony before anything happens. Release her now."

The agent smirked. "Only the president of the United States can reverse this." He handed the captain some papers.

The captain quickly read the papers and then balled them up.

"You can get out of my way now," the agent said. When the captain moved, the agent closed his door and drove off with Sonia.

***

Across the city, at Casey's penthouse apartment on the North Side, he was getting the same visit from the police as Sonia did. Since he had a doorman and the police had to climb several floors to get to his apartment door, he had ample time to get ready. When the police knocked on his door, he didn't bother asking who it was or anything else to stall. He just opened up.

"Okay, let's go downtown. My attorney is heading there now," he said, smiling at the officers.

Like Sonia, when they got downstairs, some government agents took custody of Casey and drove away with him.

***

Back in Sea Islands, Lincoln and Sydney reached the hospital room of Uncle Terrence. When they walked inside, they were surprised to see him sitting up on the bed, eating ice cream and watching TV.

"Lincoln, Sydney, how you guys doing?" Terrence asked as they both went to his side and gave him a hug.

"You are doing surprisingly well. You just got shot about twelve hours ago," Sydney said, looking at him closely.

"I feel like I wasn't even shot. Feels more like muscle cramps or someone punched me."

"This is crazy," Lincoln said, astonished by his progress, too.

Terrence turned the TV volume to mute. "Where exactly are we? I've never heard of Sea Islands General Hospital in Chicago, or any area around Chicago."

Sydney and Lincoln stared at one another.

73

"Don't speak at once," Terrence said, staring at them.

"Well, Unc, I don't know how to say this, but…"

"We're in another universe," Sydney said before Lincoln could finish his sentence.

"Are you high?" Terrence asked, looking at Lincoln to see if he was in agreement with her.

"Unc, it seems like the truth. There is some weird shit going on here. Isn't this what you were talking about?"

"Earlier I was watching some news channel called SINN. All the newscasters were black, just like the hospital staff. The news was talking about America and some Sea Islands maybe heading to war over land rights. America wants this Sea Islands to tear down their wall. I thought it was a movie, but then it went to reporting the news and sports just like every news station does. Where are we?"

"Sea Islands," Sydney said.

"What are these Sea Islands?" Terrence asked, trying to get a clear understanding of things.

"It's a country that includes part of the Southeast United States we know and other countries, such as Puerto Rico and Cuba," Lincoln said. "My father and mother can tell us more later."

There was a deafening silence in the room as Terrence processed what Lincoln had just said.

"Are you fucking crazy?" he said, laughing in Sydney's direction, thinking she was in on the joke, too.

"This is no joke," Sydney said.

"My father is the king of Sea Islands. My DNA test set all this stuff in motion. Apparently, when you found me, it was a meeting gone wrong, where my father was trying to help America with new ideas from Sea

Islands, but our government only wanted to steal the technology and treat us like aliens."

"Your parents are alive?"

Lincoln nodded. "It looks that way."

"Damn, so, you are saying that your father is the king of this Sea Islands place?"

"Yeah."

"So, where are your parents now?"

"The castle."

Terrence smiled. "Yeah, I still don't know about this shit. Seems too far-fetched for me."

"You said the plane took off like it wasn't from this planet," Lincoln replied.

"I say a lot of things. That was a figure of speech. I didn't say I believed any of it."

"I'm not sure what to believe myself," Sydney chimed in. "He even got a wife in waiting. Chick from Kenya."

"A wife in waiting?" Terrence laughed. "This sounds like some *Coming to America* shit."

"In Sea Islands, a guy can have two wives. Lincoln and this chick have been aligned to get married since birth."

"Two wives? I could learn to like it here. Who is she, and who is her family?" Terrence asked. "Must be powerful."

"She's Kenyan royalty. She was waiting on us when we got there."

Sydney smirked. "No, the heifer was waiting on you, not me. Get the story right."

"Yeah, it's all crazy, but if they ask or bring it up, Sydney is my wife."

Terrence rolled his eyes. "And the plot thickens. What are your parents like?"

Lincoln bit his lip. "I'm not sure what to think right now. My mother seems cool, but my father...I'm not sure at all what's up with that dude."

"When are we going back?"

Sydney and Lincoln stared at one another once more.

Terrence put down the ice cream. "I'm tired of this 'secret look' shit. Give it to me straight."

"I'm not sure when we can go back, or even if we can," Lincoln said with fear on his face.

"I'm going back to Chicago," Terrence said forcefully. "No one is running me out of my city."

"Me, either," Sydney said. "That's home for me."

Lincoln looked at both of them. "People are trying to kill us there. The government knows who I am. You two are connected to me. You think we can waltz back into Chicago and nothing will happen? Uncle Terrence, you almost died. What happened, anyway? How did they catch you?"

Terrence took a deep breath. "All I remember was coming out of the station and getting into my car. A black lady tapped on my window. She said she knew your parents and needed to see you urgently. We were heading to the Navy Pier, but at the light, we got cornered and taken to my house by two white guys with military-grade weapons. I heard one of the people say something about making it look like a double homicide or something like that. They shot the woman first because she wouldn't tell them anything. Then they shot me. That's all I remember."

"They tried to kill you at the hospital, too. You saw the men?" Sydney asked.

"Yeah, I saw them, two white guys. I remember their faces. They better hope they don't see me when I get back."

"Are you even listening? How can we go back and not get probed by the government like we're at Area 51?"

"Where is Sonia at?" Terrence asked, ignoring Lincoln's question.

"Oh, God, don't remind me. She's gonna kill me when I get back."

Sydney laughed. "I see we're not the only ones who need to go back home."

"I'm going back home, but I just want things to be normal. I don't want to live on the run," Lincoln declared.

"Maybe it's not that bad," said Terrence. "I saw who shot me. We find them and find out who's behind it. Simple police math."

"I'm not sure it's that easy, Unc."

David came to the doorway, and he stood there, waiting for them to notice him. Lincoln saw him from the corner of his eye.

"Hey, David, what's going on?" he asked.

Terrence looked at Lincoln and Sydney, waiting for one of them to introduce him.

Lincoln saw his uncle's slit eyes. "Hey, David, this is my uncle Terrence."

David and Terrence locked eyes. Both men were suspicious of the other.

"I hope our hospital staff has been treating you well. I told them you are a special friend of the king," said David.

Terrence looked at Lincoln and Sonia and then stared back at David. "What's really going on here? Why are we here?"

"You are here because your government was about to kill you and the heir to our country. Thank God we got to you guys before they did."

"So, when can we go back?" Lincoln asked.

David sighed. "Going back isn't safe for any of you right now, or maybe even ever. Your government is after you and wants answers. They will not accept 'I don't know' as a response."

"I can't stay here forever. I got a life and a job in Chicago," Sydney said with frustration.

"Aren't you going to stay here with your husband?" David asked.

Sydney and Lincoln looked at each other.

"Hey, David, I understand you are trying to do your job, and that's cool, but we don't need a babysitter. I have no problem dealing with our government. Just some more red tape. They have nothing on either of us. They will ask us questions, and we will tell them exactly what we know, and that's nothing. We don't know how we got here, and we're not telling anyone that we even came here. We'll go back and say we ran because we thought someone was trying to kill my uncle and me. They can't convict us of anything if we don't know anything," Lincoln stared at David.

David looked at Sonia and Terrence. "You two can go back if you please. I will make accommodations for your travel tomorrow. Lincoln, I think it is in your best interest to stay and talk to your father and mother before you leave."

"Am I ready for travel?" Terrence asked.

"We have the best surgeons in the world here. Our surgeons have a very advanced healing process that closes up the body and reconnects all the torn tissues back to the normal state in a matter of minutes. No nation or universe has our capabilities, at least none we have found. As you can see, there are no stitches."

"Are there other universes out there besides this and where we come from?" Sydney asked.

"No. We have been researching for a while and have not found a trace of another universe."

Terrence placed his hand under his gown and felt no stitches. "What did you do? Use Super Glue?"

"We saved your life and advanced the healing process. You are free to go now. It will feel like a body ache or cramp for a few days, and then you will return to normal."

"Man, something's not right," Terrence said, stretching his arms and getting out of bed to walk. He wobbled briefly and then stood up. "Shit, I need to take your hospital to Chicago."

"Where is my father now?" Lincoln asked.

"The king is waiting for you to return. I know you probably don't trust him, or any of us, but we have your best interest at heart. You're the heir to the throne. This country needs you more than anything right now."

"I'm nobody. Just a kid from Chicago."

"But you're a kid from Sea Islands and the son of royalty, and that makes you special."

"I will talk to him, but there's nothing he can say that will have me stay here while my people leave. We came together, and that's the way we will be leaving."

David smiled. "Sir, I will be waiting downstairs when you all are ready to go back to the mansion." He turned and walked away.

Lincoln looked at Sydney and Terrence. "Should we be concerned about going back to Chicago?"

"The chief will help us out. He's been like a brother to me," Terrence said. "We have nothing to worry about back home. They will see that this is just a big misunderstanding. Just don't mention the universe shit. We might end up in an asylum if that gets out."

"I agree," Sydney said. "This place is starting to seem creepy. Gunshots gone after not even a day and no stitches. Something is definitely off here."

Terrence rubbed where he had been shot. "I'm not sure about the creepy part, but damn, they did a hell of a job on my gunshot wounds. I feel good." He stretched his body again.

Sydney saw the concern on Lincoln's face. "Are you worried about something happening in Chicago when we get back?"

"I don't know. I just wish I knew what was going on before we went back. I hate going in blindly."

***

From outside the old abandoned Manteno State Hospital, about ninety miles from downtown Chicago, it seemed like an isolated and crumbling building, but beneath the deterioration in the basement was an advanced government intelligence office. The basement offices had about twenty-five people working and monitoring different suspected alien activities across the country. Down the long corridor were two rooms; one had Casey in it, and the other had Sonia. The only thing that separated the two was a glass window, which allowed them to see each other, but they weren't able to hear one another.

Sonia was handcuffed to a table, facing the window to Casey's room. With her were Special Agents Maggie Jones and Darren Mitchell. Agent Jones was a light-skinned black woman in her late forties, and Agent Mitchell was a white male in his early forties. They had been partners for the last twelve years in the OSI (Outer Space Intelligence) Agency. In the other room, with his hands tied behind his back, Casey was getting beaten and tortured by three other agents while Sonia watched.

"We don't know anything!" she cried as she tried to turn away from looking, but Agent Jones held her head so that she saw everything that was happening to Casey.

"So, you think we believe that your boyfriend just up and disappeared without letting you know what was going on?" Agent Mitchell yelled in her face. "Look at him good. If we don't get the answers out of you now, then it will be you in his place. Somebody is going to talk, or somebody is going to die."

"I know my rights. I'm an attorney. I want out of here now!" Sonia demanded.

Agent Jones stopped holding her head and looked over at Agent Mitchell with a smile. "This bitch actually thinks she gets an attorney. Want a phone call next? Maybe a soda and snack from the snack machine> Anything else, Ms. Thang, to make your stay here more comfortable?"

"I'm going to sue the hell out of you guys," Sonia said, darting her eyes at Agent Jones. "Bitch, you don't know me."

Agent Jones unleashed a fury of slaps across Sonia's face. She only stopped because Agent Mitchell grabbed her. Sonia bled from her mouth as tears raced down her face. A lump formed in her throat as she glanced over at Casey, who appeared to be barely holding on, as the agents in the other room were now waterboarding him with a towel covering his face.

"What do you want to know?" Sonia asked.

"We've been here for over three hours, and you are asking me now what we want? Are you remedial?" Agent Jones raised her hand as if she wanted to hit Sonia again. Sonia, though in handcuffs, tried to cover her face out of fear of being struck again. Agent Jones smiled, knowing that she now had beaten fear into Sonia. "Where are Lincoln Douglas and his uncle Terrence? And don't say, 'I don't know,' again."

Sonia looked up at Agent Jones and Mitchell and then across at Casey. "After the shooting at the hospital, Lincoln got a call from Sydney."

"Who is Sydney?" Agent Mitchell asked, looking through his file. He pulled out a picture and placed it in front of Sonia. "Is she in this picture?"

Sonia stared at the picture, which showed Lincoln and Sydney getting on the plane as Terrence was being carried in on a stretcher. She gritted her teeth, infuriated at the sight of Lincoln and Sydney getting on the plane.

"She's a cop in his uncle's department. Whatever you are looking for, she's at the center of it all. She called him. He told me to get off on the first floor and wait on him. I got off, and he went to the basement to meet her. I think she had his uncle and something happened. I'm not sure if his uncle was dying or what. He left me at the front and then called and told me to go home. And that's the last time I was in contact with him. Casey over there doesn't know anything. He wasn't even at the hospital or in this picture. Besides Lincoln, Sydney, and Terrence, I have never seen these people. What is this really about?"

"Ms. Sonia, either you're a great actress or a dumb girlfriend. We believe Lincoln Douglas might be an alien from another planet," Agent Mitchell said, staring at her and waiting for her reaction.

"You got to be joking! All of this because you think he's an alien? Lincoln's no outer-space alien or illegal alien from Mexico. This is ridiculous."

Agent Jones pulled out her iPad and played a video for Sonia. In the video, the plane's hatch closed, and the plane took off into the air. Seconds later, it vanished into the night. Sonia couldn't believe it herself, but she assumed it was Agent Jones trying to play mind games with her.

"There has to be a reasonable explanation here. Lincoln is no alien. I have known him for years. Hell, Casey and him grew up together."

"What has he told you about his parents and what happened to them?" Agent Mitchell asked.

"They died when he was like four or five years old."

Agent Jones pulled a chair up alongside Sonia. "I bet he never told you his uncle Terrence isn't really a blood relative."

Sonia did her best to conceal her shocked expression. "So, he was adopted?"

Agent Mitchell and Jones both chuckled.

"Here's the thing, Sonia. Lincoln's parents are alive and living," Agent Mitchell said.

"Does he know?" Sonia asked.

"Yeah, he does know about his parents here in the US, but the funny thing about it all is that these parents have never met or donated sperm or been a part of some testing. It's like Lincoln is a miracle baby, but with these people's DNA. Don't you think that's odd?"

Sonia assumed the agents were lying. "Lincoln would have told me about his parents."

"You know, until now, I see that you didn't know Lincoln at all," Agent Jones said with a devilish smile. "He has been keeping all kinds of secrets from you."

"Lincoln loves me."

"Apparently not enough." Agent Jones rolled her eyes at Sonia.

"What do you want from me?" Sonia begged. "I just want to go home."

Agent Mitchell unlocked her handcuffs, and then he went over to the door and opened it. Sonia didn't know what to think. She stared at both of the agents and then back over at Casey.

"What about him?" she asked.

"Good question," Agent Jones said. "He's staying here, but you're bringing Lincoln back here."

"How am I going to do that? I don't know where he went."

"He's a guy with a heart. Lincoln will be back to either have you go back with him or maybe to come back to stay, but he will come back," Agent Mitchell said with a smirk.

"And what if I can't?" Sonia asked.

Agent Jones pulled out her iPad again and pushed play on it. This video showed Sonia's parents tied up in what looked like a prison cell.

Sonia placed her face in her hands and cried. "They don't have anything to do with this. I'll do whatever you want. Just let them go. Please!" she said. "I'm begging you."

Agent Jones grabbed her walkie talkie and spoke into it. "She's coming down now. Make sure she has everything we need to catch him." She turned back to Sonia. "If you love your parents or Casey, you want to bring Lincoln back here. The alternative for you isn't a good ending at all."

Sonia stood up and walked to the door, where Agent Mitchell was waiting.

"Right down the hallway, through those doors, the techs will be waiting on you. And don't tell anybody you know or call the police. We have eyes everywhere," Agent Mitchell said.

As Sonia slowly walked down the long hallway, she occasionally glanced back. She thought about the video of the plane taking off. Though she still couldn't believe what the agents had told her about Lincoln, she did think there had to be some truth in what they had said.

"Lincoln, what are you hiding?" she said to herself as she opened the door at the end of the hallway.

Back inside the room where Casey was being waterboarded, the agents stopped and removed the towel. Agent Jones walked into the room and stood over him. After several minutes, Casey was able to catch his breath and look into the other room. Not seeing Sonia, he feared the worst had happened to her.

trailblazer. I shouldn't have taken you with us. You're too valuable to this nation."

Lincoln shook his head. "I don't know this nation or you. Half this shit, I don't even believe. This might be some elaborate production."

Both men laughed loudly.

"Yeah, I guess that would be crazy. All of this for a prank, but this doesn't seem real to me," Lincoln said, looking into Jasani's eyes.

Jasani smiled. "I understand. We can't turn back the clock, but we also can't stop the clock from moving forward. You're home now. This is where you belong. Your mother needs you here. I need you here."

Lincoln slit his eyes at Jasani. "And why is that?" It's not just the war with America. It's something else."

As Jasani glared at his son, tears filled his eyes. "As advanced as our country is, we still haven't found a cure for cancer."

"Damn, I'm sorry," Lincoln said with sympathy as he looked at his father. "How long does she have?"

"Not her. I'm just glad I found you before I died. I promised your mother that I wouldn't stop until I did. She doesn't know about the cancer."

"You haven't told her?"

"No, I can't until I convince you to stay and become king."

Lincoln wiped a tear away from his eye. "I can't stay. I got a life back there that I like. I have no idea how to run a country, let alone a royal family or royal council."

"That life is over. If you go back, you will be on the run until they catch you and torture you to death."

Lincoln thought about this. "Who was that woman here earlier?"

"You mean Dalilah. She's a beautiful woman," Jasani said. "You like her?"

"What is her purpose? I want you to be truthful."

Jasani was hesitant about revealing the truth, but he gave in as he knew the truth was probably the only chance he had of getting Lincoln to even consider staying.

"Her father is the king of Kenya in Africa. They and Canada are our strongest allies. I need him, and your union with her is vital to our survival."

"Unbelievable," Lincoln said, stunned. "What were you going to do if I didn't come back?"

"I would have had a choice but to marry her myself, but that would have left our nation vulnerable to Africa taking control of us once I died. I need a successor who will not only watch over the nation, but our family as well."

Lincoln got up and paced the floor. He looked over at Jasani, who stared back at him. "How did this different-universe stuff happen in the first place? It seems impossible. How do you travel back and forth?"

"Oh, this all started with Zebadiah Douglas. He was the first free Douglas. In 1861, he was hired to be Simon Newcomb's assistant at the United States Naval Observatory in Washington, D.C. Simon had Zebadiah looking into the motion of the planets as they moved through the universe. Zebadiah loved it and studied as much as possible. Simon Newcomb even took him to Ireland to see what was, at the time, the world's largest telescope, built by William Parsons. They came back, and Zebadiah and Simon built their own telescope. Not as big, but it did the job."

"So, a telescope did all this?" Lincoln asked with a confused look.

"Don't rush history. I'm getting to it."

"Sorry." Lincoln came back over to the couch and sat down.

"So, one night, while Zebadiah was working, he noticed what looked like a wrinkle or hole in the sky that he could only see through the telescope. He ran and showed Simon. Simon saw it, too. They went and told President Lincoln. He thought they were crazy. Simon and Zebadiah wouldn't give up, so they went and paid for a hot-air balloon because that was the only way to travel in the sky at that time."

***

April 13, 1864, just outside of Washington, D.C., Zebadiah jumped into the hot-air balloon. Simon handed him different items to place inside it before requesting help to climb aboard. Zebadiah helped him in and started the flame. As he began untying the ropes from the stakes in the ground, Simon stopped him.

"Are you sure you can fly this?" Simon asked, looking into the night sky.

Zebadiah looked at the flame and then into the sky himself. He got out the small telescope out of his jacket pocket and looked at the sky again. "I can do it," he said, untying the rest of the ropes. He knew that they were either going to make it or die, so no matter what, Simon would either be happy or dead.

The hot-air balloon flew up into the sky as Zebadiah did his best to navigate it toward the wrinkle he had seen through the telescope. As they traveled higher and higher into the sky, both men were nervous and scared, but neither said a word about it. Being their first time piloting a hot air balloon by themselves, every little jerk or strong wind intensified the moment even more. From the flush look on Simon's normally pale face, Zebadiah could tell that his companion was getting sick.

"Are you okay?" Zebadiah asked. He wasn't feeling that great, either.

Simon forced a smile. "I'll survive."

Zebadiah looked through his pocket telescope again. "We're almost there."

Simon grabbed the telescope and took a look. He saw the wrinkle, but it was like a hole in the sky that could only be seen through a telescope of some kind. Zebadiah navigated them over to the hole. He and Simon looked at one another one last time as they entered the hole.

"God will protect us," Zebadiah said as the hole sucked the hot-air balloon in and twirled them through like they were as thin as paper. Both Simon and Zebadiah held on for dear life. Both men assumed this was their ride to death. It seemed like they twisted and twirled for hours on end, but in actuality, it was only thirty minutes.

When it all stopped, the hot-air balloon went back to normal, floating like it had been before they'd been sucked into the hole. The sky looked the same, as did the buildings and land below them. To Simon and Zebadiah, it looked like nothing had changed.

"I guess this was a non-event," Simon said, giving Simon a somewhat-disappointed look.

"It just seems weird that the sky did all that for us to come back right where we started." Zebadiah glanced around at their surroundings.

Simon smirked. "I think I'll take over the measuring of the movements of the planets when we get back. I've got other duties for you."

Zebadiah was hurt. He knew Simon was putting the blame for the failed mission solely on his shoulders. He wanted to defend his stance, but he knew, as a black man in the 1860s, that he would be putting himself in a very sticky situation if he were to accuse a white man of anything. So, he stayed quiet and tended to landing the hot-air balloon.

When they landed, Zebadiah turned off the flame and jumped out to tie the ropes to the ground. Both men glanced back up at the sky, wondering what had gone wrong. Then they noticed that their horse carriage was not where they had left it.

"Immediately after you and Mr. Newcomb convince your President Lincoln of what has happened. Then all four of us will need to head back and convince our President Lincoln."

"Your thoughts are rightly aligned with mine," Sir Simon said as he rested his head back, too.

Zebadiah went over to Zee. "I hope this works tomorrow."

"It has to. Lincoln should see this as a great opportunity for him and the rest of the universe," Zee said with hesitation. "But we do have to be prepared for him saying no."

"Why?" Zebadiah asked.

"Just because we believe it and know it's possible, it doesn't mean he will."

"What else can we do?" Zee asked.

"Exactly nothing. Hopefully, they present the case right, and things go as planned."

"I'm going to get some shut-eye downstairs. See you in the morning," Zebadiah said as he walked out of the room.

***

The next morning came soon, and all four men stood in the hallway, waiting to meet with President Lincoln. They waited for about an hour. Many people who passed by Lincoln's office commented on the four men and how they looked like each other.

When they walked into the office, the first thing Lincoln did was burst out laughing. He assumed it was a joke of sorts.

"I didn't know you had such a personality, Simon," he said, still giggling at the sight of all four men. "I say, that a great trick."

"It's no trick, Mr. President. And we are not related in the normal way," Sir Simon said.

Lincoln stopped what he was doing and took a closer look at the four men. "What are you alluding to, Simon?"

Mr. Newcomb went and stood in front of Lincoln's desk. "You remember when I came by and we discussed that wrinkle in the night sky and you thought it was crazy talk? That wrinkle leads to another universe. That's where he and Zebadiah come from. Last night, they came through a hole in the sky to our world."

Lincoln looked at Mr. Newcomb, waiting for the punchline. When it didn't come, he stood up and paced the floor. The four men stared at each other, wondering what the president was thinking.

"Are you okay, Mr. President?" Sir Simon asked.

"So, right now, there's another President Lincoln, my twin, who is pacing this office floor but in a different universe?"

The men all looked at each other again.

"No, Mr. President," Zebadiah said. "Since we are here, there is no one telling you about traveling through the universe."

"We will need to convince him as well of the two universes. But it all has to happen soon so that we do not affect the different timelines of our worlds too much," Zee said looking at the president. "You understand, Mr. President?"

Lincoln smiled. "I got it. I want to see it for myself. I've always had a fascination with the stars."

"You want to travel in a hot-air balloon with all four of us?" Sir Simon said, trying to figure out if the president was serious or not.

"The best way to convince this other President Lincoln is to bring me. I will be able to answer any question he asks. I know him like he knows me. We will go tomorrow night."

"Mr. President, time is very sensitive. The longer we are here with you, the more our universe loses alignment with yours," Sir Simon said, hoping the president understood where he was coming from.

"Understood, but that's the only way this is happening. I have a play I'm going to tonight with Mary and General Grant and his wife. Tomorrow we can disappear, and no one will care. I'll tell Mary that I'm getting on a train to New York City."

Though the men didn't want to wait, they knew that to get Lincoln's buy-in, he had to make the trip with them.

"Tomorrow night it is, Mr. President," Mr. Newcomb said as the others nodded in agreement.

"We'll disappear tomorrow night after supper. Meet me at the back door, and I will have my guard take us to where we need to be. I'm assuming that's going to be the hot-air balloon." Lincoln chuckled. "Good day, gentlemen."

The four men walked out of the Oval Office, looking dejected but optimistic.

***

Back in 2025, at the king's castle, Jasani was still talking to Lincoln about the history of Sea Islands and how it came to be.

"So, what happened?" Lincoln asked, deep into the history lesson.

"Well, the night Abraham Lincoln went to the play, his wife, Mary, cast doubt on who the men were. He ended up switching seats because he couldn't stop talking about us and the different universe. The assassin came in and shot Major Rathbone instead of President Lincoln. Lincoln lived, which then made it clear for the forty acres to be given to former slaves and freemen. From that point forward, black people created their own independence based on the white race believing they were superior to other nations. We joined forces with the inferior nations and became the superior nation."

"You've told me this story before. It's not just a crazy dream," Lincoln said, amazed that he remembered.

"Yeah, I used to read the book of our history to put you to sleep at night. I figured that it was boring enough for you to fall asleep. We also have several movies made about it as well."

"Did it work?"

"You falling asleep?" Jasani smiled. "Every time."

"So, what happened to Simon Newcomb and Zebadiah Douglas?"

Jasani frowned. "I hate this part of the story. It's the reason our worlds are so different."

"So, what happened?"

"Well, President Lincoln survived. The next day, the Simon and Zebadiah from this world went to meet the president while the other Simon and Zebadiah went to get the hot-air balloon to get ready for their voyage. Apparently, Lincoln had second thoughts about what they had told him the day before, and he had them arrested for being a part of some type of assassination plot."

"What?" Lincoln was shocked.

"Yeah, that was pretty sad. They were accused of being secret agents for the Confederate Army. Our Simon turned against Zebadiah in court. Zebadiah was hung for telling the truth. Simon said that it was all a parlor trick. Lincoln tried hard to find the other men, but they got away. The other Zebadiah did return years later, after Lincoln was no longer in office, and lived out the rest of his life in Florida."

"So, Douglasville is named after him?"

"No, it's named after Jean Douglas, his youngest brother and my great-great-grandfather. He was given land in the Special Field Order No.

15, which they gave to newly freed black families. We avoided the scandal with Henry Cooke stealing our money from the Freeman's Bank by managing it ourselves. Why would we let a white man manage black money? Those two things destroyed the black people in your world."

Lincoln scowled. "Yeah, I agree. That set us back at least a century and a half. People always thinking black people are asking for free money when reparations are mentioned. Reparations are for what was stolen from us and that doesn't even include the slave labor."

"Your world is not a kind place."

Lincoln nodded. "So, what did Jean Douglas do to build all of this?"

"He built up Sea Islands by buying land and building his own empire. Zebadiah helped him navigate how his world worked, and they used it to build what we see today. Instead of a democracy, we built a monarchy for the Douglas family since we own like seventy-five percent of all the land."

"That's a lot. Did the other Simon Newcomb ever come back?"

"Yeah, but once he found out what had happened to the Simon in this world, he returned and pretended like this was all made-up lies on Zebadiah's part. That was why Zebadiah came back here and never returned to that universe."

"Man, that's a lot to absorb."

"That's why I want you to stay. I want you to learn about your heritage and your family. You haven't even met your sisters yet."

"I'm sure they are on the fence about me," Lincoln said with one eye on his father.

"They are dying to meet their brother. They wanted to come over tonight, but I told them to wait until tomorrow so that I can introduce you to the world here."

"What do you mean by 'introduce me to the world'? So, everyone in this world knows about your trips to our universe?"

"No, only a small group of people know, and they are all vetted and work directly for me. They are the most trusted people in Sea Islands. Your sisters don't even know about it. Only people with royal council security clearance have access to this information. If someone outside of my inner circle were to find out, they would be executed. Make sure Sydney and Terrence keep quiet as well."

Lincoln saw the seriousness on his father's face. "So, what is the story behind me coming back?"

"You were kidnapped and grew up in Europe. Our Europe. For the past ten years, you have been in Chicago, working as a police detective. I had my information technician create a record for you and Sydney just in case someone decides to go snooping."

"What about my uncle Terrence?"

Jasani smiled at Lincoln. "Funny thing about him is that even in this world, he ended up being a police officer in Chicago. His life is drastically different, but he's probably happier."

"He has a family?"

"Yes, but I caution him and Sydney about researching themselves here. It could alter lives."

"America here has no clue about your capabilities?"

"They refuse to believe it. They would handle the discovery the same way your universe handles it: by trying to steal instead of working with you. To them, this would be a weapon that they could use against us."

Lincoln nodded. He knew Jasani was right. "How big is this introduction thing?"

"Just a small gathering of people. Some press."

Lincoln sighed. "My people want to leave tomorrow. Is that a problem?"

"Son, if, after the introduction and meeting your sisters, you still want to leave, I will have you and them back in Chicago before tomorrow midnight."

"Cool."

"How long have you and Sydney been married?"

Lincoln mustered up a smile and then looked away from Jasani. "A few years. We met on the job."

"You two are police officers, right?"

"Yes."

"Very honorable. I hate that we lost you all those years ago." Jasani turned away from his son. He felt like he had let him down.

"Can't change the past," Lincoln said, trying to make his father feel more at ease with everything that had occurred years ago.

"But if you leave, we have no future."

Both men sat across from each other, thinking about the words they had just exchanged.

"If Lincoln killed Zee, then why did you name me Lincoln?"

Jasani smiled. "President Lincoln is the reason there is a Sea Islands. He didn't kill Zebadiah. The people did that. Mr. Newcomb did that. He had a chance to prove the universe theory, but he chose to lie and let Zee die in the process. Lincoln was just a non-believer. But his commitment to his promise and his wanting to keep the white race from what they termed 'native people' is why we are more powerful and scare the hell out of them today. I've seen what black people have gone through in your world. Here, we never needed a Rosa Parks or Martin Luther King Jr. Lincoln's life altered our universe for the good of black people. We own our own culture. No one profits off of Sea Islands like the white man does in your world."

99

"It all just seems weird," Lincoln said.

"Your name is not meant to really honor him, but to remember him and how we really started. Your name is the alpha and omega of this universe. It started with Lincoln, and will someday end with a Douglas in charge."

Lincoln thought about his father's words and it finally made sense to him. "I now get it. For all these years, I always thought I was named after him because he freed the slaves. I also imagined I was related to Frederick Douglas growing up."

"You are."

"That's impressive," Lincoln said with a smile. "What was he like in your history books?"

"Hated by many. His love for white women almost destroyed us."

"Ouch," Lincoln said with his eyes wide open.

Jasani looked at his watch. It was now three o'clock in the morning. "Whoa! It's late. We need to be up and dressed by nine."

"Is this for the welcoming event?"

"No, that's at noon. Nine o'clock is the family breakfast. We will all gather, and your family will get to meet you and your wife, Sydney."

"Is there a store open early in the morning where we can buy some things to wear? I need shower products, and I'm sure Sydney does as well."

Jasani beamed at him. "That is all taken care of. In your bedroom upstairs, you will find that the two of you and your uncle have plenty of options for the breakfast and the introduction ceremony."

"How do you even know our sizes?" Lincoln asked, confused.

"Son, when we discovered that you were still alive, we did a lot of research on you and your uncle." Jasani stared at Lincoln. "But we didn't find any information indicating a wife in your life. Your mother, after meeting Sydney had several items picked out from our top designers. I think she will be very pleased."

"Will that other girl be at the breakfast and ceremony?"

"Dalilah is her name, and yes, she will be there. She is our invited guest and was to be your wife."

"And when I leave, her father will look at it as a betrayal of your relationship, and your two countries will be at odds. Unless you take her as a wife. Things are definitely different in my world. That's called polygamy, and that is illegal. People get arrested for that."

"That's an interesting take on marriage. But don't worry about that, son. I will cross that bridge when we get to it. I know your mother will be devastated with you leaving, but I will try to make her understand your decision."

Lincoln saw the hurt in his father's eyes. He wished he could tell him that he would stay, but he knew Sydney and Terrence were ready to head back to their world in Chicago. "It's not like I'm not coming back. I'll be back often as I can. I'm not going to lose you guys again. Don't worry about that."

Jasani smirked. "The portal isn't like catching a bus. A lot of coordination goes into making sure things go off right. Like, after a while, we will need to change our entry point, especially with people looking for you. They are going to search all of Chicago to find that entry point."

"Yeah, I didn't think about it like that."

Jasani went and gave his son a passionate hug. He feared the worst would happen when Lincoln returned to his universe.

Jasani wiped his eyes. "Son, get some sleep, and I'll see you first thing in the morning."

They broke from the embrace.

"Yeah, definitely. Which room is mine?" Lincoln asked as he walked toward the door.

"Upstairs to the right, three doors down. The door has your name on it. If you change your mind and stay, the residence next door is yours as well."

"And Sydney is already in there?" Lincoln asked, surprised that things were so efficient.

Jasani slit his eyes at Lincoln. "Where else would your wife be sleeping?"

"No, no, that's good. See you in the morning," Lincoln said, and then he left the office.

As the door closed behind him, Jasani pushed a button on his desk. Within a matter of seconds, David came into the room through another door.

"Yes, King Jasani," David said.

"Tonight, Lincoln, Sydney, and Terrence will be going back."

David looked surprised. "So soon, King."

"It is his wish for now. I must honor it."

"Is that a wise decision? They will be picked up and tortured into giving information about our world, which they don't know."

"David, that's why I want you to assemble a team to be on alert to go and get him when he is captured. I need my son captured first and then rescued. He needs to understand the risk of him trying to live back in that world. That's the only way I can convince him to stay here. So, tonight, when the plane goes back, I want you to drop them off and make sure they are safe, and then wait for my signal. If we have to destroy Chicago to save him, we will."

"Yes, sir. I'll get everything in order."

"Thanks, David. Keep this between us."

"I wouldn't see it any other way, your highness. Is there anything else you need, your majesty?"

Jasani shook his head. "No. You have a good night, David."

David turned and left the room through the door he had entered. Jasani sat back down at his desk and stared off into space.

***

Lincoln walked into the bedroom. He saw Sydney sleeping, and he smiled at how beautiful and peaceful she looked. He wanted to join her in bed, but he knew that would change their relationship forever. He went inside the massive walk-in closet and looked at the clothes.

"Damn, these are nice," he said as he flicked through them, chuckling to himself. "I'm not sure my taste is this good." He sat down on the bench in the middle of the closet and tried on a pair of shoes. "Damn, these fit perfectly. Shit, maybe I should pack a bag to go."

Lincoln took the shoes off and was walking out of the closet when he came nose to nose with Sydney. He was shocked that she was up. They stared into each other's eyes, hoping the other would make the first move, but neither did.

"You have beautiful eyes," Lincoln said, praying that she would lean forward and kiss him. With her knowing about Sonia, he didn't want to make the first move because he wasn't sure how she would react.

Sydney rolled her eyes playfully to break the awkward moment. "Nothing special about these eyes." She exhaled.

"You see the clothes?" Lincoln asked.

"Man, I was thinking about how I could take some of these back with me. I don't like stealing, but damn, I'm tempted."

"I know, right?"

"You know you can stay. Terrence and I can go back by ourselves. You need to get to know your parents better. This would have been your life if you had never been lost."

"I wish I could see how I turned out in this world," Sydney said, her eyes filled with curiosity.

"I'm sure a stripper or something close to that," he joked. "But don't. My father, the king, cautioned me about you doing that. Something about altering the future of yourself here."

"I get it. Part of me would love to stay and see more of what this world is like. It seems like black people are in a better position."

"So, now you want to stay? You like being my wife, huh?"

She playfully pushed him in the chest. "I'm twisted. I want to go back, but I'm open to relocating to the nearest universe to me," she said, laughing. "If you want to stay, I wouldn't hold it against you. You're part of a royal family."

Lincoln contemplated what she had just said. He did want to stay, but he didn't want to break away from the group. "Yeah, I think that would be kind of awkward for my wife to go back without me."

"Dang, I forgot about that."

"And if I stayed back, I would probably have to marry Dalilah."

"Ouch," Sydney said with a chuckle.

"Yeah, I need to go back."

"For Sonia," Sydney said, looking into his eyes. Though she had expected the answer to be yes, her heart had been hoping for no to come out of his mouth.

"That's part of the reason. I need to make sure she's okay. Even Casey might be in trouble. If they are really after me, then they probably went after the people closest to me."

"If that's the case, then I am glad I came with you. I don't have time to get tortured like a war criminal." She laughed. "It's bad for my hair and nails."

"We better get to bed."

"I'm sleeping in until we leave," Sydney said, yawning.

"Yeah, that's not going to happen."

"Why not?" Sydney raised her eyebrow.

"Well, the family is having a breakfast tomorrow. Everyone will be there. And being my wife, you are expected to be there. Also, the universe travel is only known by my mother, my father, and key members of the royal council, who report directly to him."

"What about your sisters?"

Lincoln raised his eyebrow at her. "They don't know, either, so definitely don't mention it."

"Who else doesn't know?"

"America," he said. "Man, that sounds funny."

"Yes, it does." They smiled at each other.

"Tomorrow, I mean, in a few hours, will definitely be interesting." Lincoln shook his head, thinking about the planned events. "I kind of hate that we lied about being married, but if I hadn't, then I'd probably be talking about my wedding in a few hours. Thanks for backing me up on that."

Sydney smiled at him. "Any other duties I need to be apprised of, my husband?"

"Shoot, I forgot. At noon tomorrow, they are doing an introduction ceremony."

"What the heck is that?" she asked.

"I'm not sure. But my father says that it's a small event. Some press."

"Doesn't sound small to me."

Lincoln smirked. "Dang, girl, you act like you got something better to do."

"We're getting an annulment right now. I'm tired," Sydney said, smiling at him.

"You think being fake-married to you is a treat?" he said, laughing as he walked into the bedroom.

"I'm the best wife you will ever have, fake or real," she said as she walked behind him. "Who has had your back more than me?"

Lincoln exhaled. "Want me to kiss your feet now or later?"

"Smart-ass!"

Lincoln went over to the couch and laid down, while Sydney went back to the bed. She glanced over at him as he tried to get comfortable.

"You know, you can sleep in the bed with me. Just don't touch my booty." She smiled at him.

Lincoln thought about it for a second. "And you think you would be the best wife for me? Damn, I'd hate to see the worst one."

She rolled her eyes. "Bring your butt over here. I can't have my man looking like his wife doesn't take care of him."

Lincoln got up from the couch and started to dance over to the bed. "Now we talking."

"Go to sleep, Lincoln," she said as she turned to face the other way. "And don't forget to turn off the lights."

Lincoln laughed to himself as he walked over and cut off the lights. He got in the bed and faced the back of her head. Sydney moved her butt toward him.

"Sorry," she said, smiling.

"You trying to start something."

"Go to sleep, Lincoln,"

Sydney laid there, almost motionless, waiting for his hands to touch her body. It wasn't until she heard him snoring that she decided to go to sleep herself.

Chapter SEVEN

The morning came rather quickly. A couple of knocks on the door, and then a note was slipped into the room under the door. Lincoln sat up, while Sydney was still quietly out. He got out of bed and saw the note. He picked it up and read it.

"Please wear formal attire for the breakfast event," he said to himself. "Breakfast event? Damn!"

He walked to Sydney's side of the bed and touched her gently. She woke up and smiled up at him.

"Hey, Lincoln."

"Hey, Sydney."

"You know you snore, right?" she said with sarcasm.

"My fake wife loves it," he said, rolling his eyes back at her. "Just got this note under the door. We have to dress up in formal attire for breakfast."

"Formal attire?"

"I know, right? Something doesn't seem right. I've never had a formal family breakfast before."

"Me, either," Sydney said, agreeing with him. "Maybe it's because we don't socialize in these circles."

"Now that explains the fancy clothes."

Sydney walked into the closet and grabbed a tan dress. "They even got the perfect shoes to match the dresses. I must say, being your fake wife does have its perks." She laughed.

Lincoln came inside the closet. "Should I wear something to match what you are wearing?"

"If you want to continue this ruse, I think that's the wise thing to do."

"I was thinking that. That's what Sonia would say."

Sydney cringed at the fact that he was comparing her to Sonia. She gathered the clothes, underwear, and shoes and placed them on the couch across from the bed.

"I'm taking a shower first," she said, going into the bathroom and closing the door.

Lincoln knew from how quickly her attitude changed that she was unhappy with what he had said. Being that it was the truth, he didn't know how to even apologize for it. He picked out a powder-blue suit, white shirt, and tan tie to wear. He was looking through the shoes when someone knocked on the door. He went and answered it, and it was his uncle Terrence, who barged his way inside. Lincoln closed the door behind him.

"What going on, Unc?"

"What the hell is this formal breakfast shit? I thought we were leaving today?" Terrence seemed paranoid. "I'm not going to be anybody's prisoner. Let's get out of here."

"We are, Unc. I talked to my father last night, and he said that after the breakfast and the introduction ceremony, we are free to head back to our world."

"No strings?" Terrence asked, staring at Lincoln with suspicion.

"No strings. We talked it all out last night, and it went great. I'll definitely be coming back here."

"What are you going to do about the wife-to-be chick?" Terrence asked with a snicker.

"I know. She'll be at breakfast today. I guess it was decided at birth that we would be married."

"What happens after you leave?"

Lincoln scratched his head. "That's an unknown mystery to me. My father said he would handle it."

"Did he say anything about their war with America?"

Lincoln quickly replayed last night's conversation in his head. "Funny that you ask. He didn't say a word about it."

"I'm surprised this America hasn't come to our universe," Terrence said.

"From what he told me, very few people know about the travel to our universe, just him, key members of his royal council, and my mother. Thinking about it, if the America here found out about that technology, they would go to our world and get all the resources possible to come here and destroy them. This is definitely black power in action."

"I didn't think about that, but you are right. Both Americas would be shell-shocked if they saw how things worked in both universes. Especially if white people where we are from saw this type of black empowerment. They would lose their minds."

They both started laughing.

"That would be crazy just to see how they would react," Lincoln said. "We better get ready."

Sydney opened the door to come back into the bedroom. She stopped and peeked over at Terrence. "Shouldn't you be dressed?"

Terrence glanced over at her and then at Lincoln. "You two would have been a great couple."

"Just friends," Lincoln said, dismissing the idea.

Sydney was a little put off by his abrupt response. "Dang, you didn't have to say it that way."

"What way?" he asked, not understanding why she felt offended.

"I know we're just friends, but you didn't have to say it that way."

Terrence smiled. "The first fight."

"Shouldn't you be getting dressed?" Lincoln said, opening up the bedroom door.

"I'm gone. I'll leave my two favorite people in both universes alone." Terrence walked out the door.

Lincoln closed it behind him.

"Did I do something wrong?" he asked as Sydney walked over to the couch with nothing but a bathrobe on.

She sat down and collected her thoughts. She wanted to tell him how she felt about him. Being rejected crossed her mind, and making their friendship awkward moving forward wasn't a risk she was willing to take while on this trip. "No, I'm fine."

Lincoln was disappointed by her response. He wanted to know where she stood with him regarding their friendship and possible romance. With her not giving him any indication, he still felt like he was fishing in the dark.

"Got it. I'll hurry up," he said, running into the shower.

As he closed the door, both of them regretted that the discussion hadn't revealed anything about their feelings for the other.

***

When Lincoln and Sydney walked into the grand ballroom on the first floor, they didn't know it was for a gala. The massive amount of well-dressed people shocked them.

"Is this our wedding reception?" she whispered to him, and they both laughed.

Ayanna and Jasani came to greet them at the door, in their royal attire and with their crowns on their heads. Jasani had on a black tuxedo, and Ayanna wore a black off-the-shoulder dress and diamonds around her neck that were blinding to look at. Sydney was impressed, and she smiled and gave Ayanna a hug. Then Jasani hugged Sydney while Ayanna grabbed Lincoln like it was their last embrace. She held him for what seemed like several minutes while tears filled her eyes.

She kissed him on the cheek and whispered in his ear, "I understand that you need to go, but never forget that this is also your home." She pulled away from him and looked at him and Sydney together. "You two will make beautiful babies together. I want to see my grandchildren."

Sydney and Lincoln glanced over at each other. Both felt bad that they were deceiving his parents.

Lincoln stared at Jasani. "I thought this was a small gathering of just our family?"

"Son, this is a small gathering of our family. I'm the oldest of seven kids. And your mother had six brothers and two sisters. Four of her brothers have already passed."

"Whoa!" Lincoln said. "That is a lot. I'm sorry for your losses."

Tears came to Ayanna's eyes again. "But this is the greatest loss. My heart is breaking again, knowing that you will be leaving us."

Her words touched him deeply, and he started to cry himself. Sydney had never seen him show this type of emotion. Seeing his sensitive side attracted her even more to him. She gently wrapped her arm around his waist to console him.

"Maybe you should stay," she said in his ear.

"No, we need to keep with the plan," he replied.

Ayanna saw the intimate moment between them and smiled. "Kiss your beautiful wife. I am so lucky to have such a beautiful daughter-in-law."

Lincoln and Sydney realized that almost everyone in the ballroom was staring at them. Though it was what they had both dreamed of, neither had dreamed of it happening this way.

"What do we do?" he asked her under his breath.

Without answering or thinking about it, Sydney turned and kissed him on the lips. At first contact, Lincoln pulled her body into his and pressed his lips against hers even more. Sydney felt the passion in his kiss and gave it right back to him. It was only a minute, but it was long enough for the ballroom attendees to see the fireworks between them. It wasn't until Jasani cleared his throat, hoping they'd stop, that they took notice and smiled at the onlookers.

"I'm sorry," Lincoln said to Sydney.

"I can't do this," she said, and she walked out of the ballroom headed back upstairs to their bedroom.

Lincoln turned to his parents. "This is an emotional time for us. I'll be right back. Go ahead and start the breakfast." With that, he went after Sydney.

Ayanna and Jasani looked at one another.

"Are we going to be grandparents?" Ayanna joyfully said, grabbing her husband's hand.

"Another heir. I have to convince him to stay."

"Jasani, you gave him your promise. Let him go. Protect him there, and he will be back. I've prayed on it."

At the ballroom entrance, Jasani saw Dalilah enter.

"I still have the America and Africa problem. And I don't have an answer for either one."

"Jasani, we have survived so much more than this. Today we celebrate the homecoming of our son. He is our focus."

Two tall, beautiful, brown-skinned women in their late twenties walked up to Jasani and Ayanna. They were identical twins and had on the same dress but in different colors, one summer pink and the other hot red. Jasani and Ayanna hugged the two of them.

"Late, as usual, girls," Jasani said. "Should have named you two Late and Later."

"Daddy, you know how long it takes to get ready for one of these events?" Nicole asked. She was the one in the hot-red dress.

"Set your alarm. Get up earlier," he replied. "You literally live five minutes from here, and that's walking in heels."

"We work hard for you," Tia said as she looked around. "Where is our brother at?"

"I hope he's late. I would love him forever if that's the case," Nicole said, laughing loudly.

Ayanna slit her eyes at the women. "No, your brother was here on time and has stepped away for a moment."

"What happened?" Tia asked.

"This is not something for your gossip column, Tia," Jasani said, frowning at her.

"His wife, Sydney, is pregnant, we think. She's very emotional. But don't say a word about it," Ayanna said to her daughters. "Let's all take our seats."

***

Lincoln slowly opened the bedroom door. He saw Sydney on the bed, crying. His heart pounded as he thought about what to say.

"Can I come in?" he asked, peeping his head inside.

Sydney quickly tried to cover up the fact that she had been crying. When she looked up at the door, she knew the cover-up act wasn't going to work with his eyes already fixed on her.

She took a deep breath. "Come on in."

Lincoln walked into the room, closing the door behind him. He went over to the bed and sat next to her feet.

Sydney was about to say something, but Lincoln spoke first.

"Hey, I'm going to put my cards on the table." Sydney's eyes perked up. "I like you a lot. Always have. It's just that our timing always seemed to be off. You were dating someone, or I was dating someone, and then I met Sonia. This trip has given me a moment to see you through a different lens. You showed me that you would be there for me no matter what happened. And this shit is exactly that. I understand that lying about being with me to my parents is wrong, but deep down, I want it to be right."

Sydney's heart stopped beating. She wasn't sure what he actually meant. "What are you saying, Lincoln?"

He grabbed her feet. "Damn, you really going to make this hard on me."

"I don't want there to be any misunderstanding with us."

115

Lincoln exhaled. "You're right. There shouldn't be. Sydney, I can't make you any promises right now, but I can tell you what's in my heart. And it's been there for a while. I don't want to ignore it anymore."

She looked into his eyes. "Your heart will do for me."

"I'm falling in love with you. I've been forcing a relationship with Sonia for all these years. Deep down, I know she's not the one for me. You are."

Sydney closed her eyes and took a deep breath. She then reopened her eyes. "I know this complicated for you. It is for me, too. You have been my homie, but I would be lying to you if I said I didn't want to be your lover."

"Maybe we should stay here?" he suggested.

Sydney smiled at him. "You can't run from Sonia or the therapist or whoever else there might be."

"How did you know about the therapist?" Lincoln asked, embarrassed by the revelation.

"I'm a police detective. I come from a long line of police officers. That's what we do. I wasn't spying on you. I just had your back."

Lincoln huffed. "I get it. I did the same to you."

They both laughed.

"Just for the record, I'm not falling for you."

"Whoa!" Lincoln said, feeling rejected a little.

She saw his reaction. "No, what I'm saying is I'm not falling for you. I've already fallen. I love you, Lincoln. Always have."

"Why didn't you say something?"

"Didn't want to get my heart broken."

Lincoln got up to go and kiss her on the bed when the door opened and Nicole and Tia walked in.

"You can save that for later, big brother," Nicole said, excited to see him.

She and Tia went over and hugged him and Sydney.

Lincoln was surprised to meet them this way. "You two are my sisters? This is great. I grew up without siblings."

"No more of that," Tia said, hugging him again. "You've been so missed all these years."

"I don't think there was ever a day Momma didn't mention you," Nicole said with a gleam in her eye. She seemed to be happy to have Lincoln as her brother.

"Daddy definitely didn't like grooming our cousin Shawn to be king one day," Tia added with an analytical appraisal of Lincoln.

"Where is Shawn now?" Lincoln asked curiously.

"I think on a vacation in Europe," Nicole said. "I know Daddy is happy he's gone. Shawn's more of a follower than a leader."

Lincoln looked at his two sisters with skepticism. He wasn't sure if they were telling him the honest truth. Nicole saw his look.

"I know this is all new to you. Being kidnapped and growing up in a foreign country must have been hard. I know I couldn't have handled it. And meeting all these new people can be too much. Probably like the first day in college."

"Something like that," he said, turning to Sydney. She stood up and looked at the two other women. "This is Sydney."

"Hi. I'm the wife," she said, extending her hand to them.

"Girl, please," Nicole said as she hugged her. "You are family. No need to be formal here."

Tia was a little bit more reserved. She gave Sydney a side shoulder hug. "We all have so much to talk about. Twenty-five years of catch-up. When did you get married? Where did you go to school? Who are your friends? Who are your enemies? I guess, since I don't see any kids here, you don't have any, so do you want them? All that good stuff," she said with a big smile.

"I guess I should have brought my diary," Lincoln replied with a chuckle.

Nicole noticed that Sydney had been crying. "Hold up, I know my brother is not upsetting you."

Sydney looked in the mirror on the other side of the room. She saw her eye makeup was smeared from crying. "Oops. Sorry. This is not Lincoln's fault. Your brother is a very special man. I'm dealing with some family issues at home."

Nicole looked at Tia and mouthed the word "pregnant" to her. Tia nodded in agreement.

"Come here, sis," said Nicole. "Let me help you out. I own the largest makeup company in the world, so I know a little about making people look good."

Sydney walked over to the mirror with Nicole.

"You own a fourth of the company. Don't let her fool you into thinking she's big time. It's actually Momma's company. Momma owns fifty percent, and we own the other half. I'm sure, with you being here, that ownership percentage is about to change."

"No, no, no, I'm not trying to be in the cosmetic business. We're police officers," Lincoln said.

Nicole pulled out her cosmetic case and started correcting the blemishes on Sydney's face.

"That will probably be changing now that you are here," Tia said.

Lincoln grimaced. From her response, he knew that neither she nor Nicole knew that he and Sydney were leaving that night.

"I think there's been some misunderstanding. We're not here to stay," Lincoln said, immediately getting a reaction from his sisters.

Nicole stopped working on Sydney's face, and Tia froze right in place.

"You got to be joking, right?" Nicole said, staring at Sydney.

Sydney glanced over at Lincoln, deferring to him.

Lincoln didn't want to address the subject, but he also didn't want the elephant in the room to get bigger as the day went by. "No joke. We will be leaving tonight. We both have jobs that we have to be at on Monday."

Tia tilted her and stared head at him. "You do know that your family is the richest family in the world, right?"

"They are?" Sydney asked, amazed by the information.

"Don't you guys keep up with the news?" Tia asked, looking at both of them with suspicion. "Are you guys joking with us?"

Lincoln shook his head. "I never knew about the money, or cared."

Tia didn't believe him. "You don't care about the money? I can't believe you want to go back and work a normal job after knowing who your family is."

"Lincoln, you're the heir to the throne. You're going to throw that away to be a police officer?" Nicole asked, not understanding the rationale behind his decision.

"I didn't grow up in this life. This is you and Tia's world."

"Duh, we live in the same world," Nicole said, rolling her eyes at him. She then turned her attention to Sydney. "Girl, you need to talk some sense into my brother. I don't understand how someone could give up so much to take the risk of getting shot on the job."

Lincoln didn't have a response and didn't want to discuss it any further. "Hey, I think we should be getting down to the breakfast," he said quickly, changing the subject.

"We're not done talking about this, big brother," Tia said. "Don't have us kidnap your wife. I bet you won't leave here without her."

Sydney glanced over at Lincoln and smiled. He turned and opened the bedroom door for them all to leave. Tia and Nicole walked by him with smirks on their faces. When Sydney got to the door, she grabbed his hand.

"I guess we can finish our discussion later," she said, kissing him on the cheek.

As they made their way down the spiral staircase, a picture of Sonia flashed in Lincoln's mind. A lump formed in his throat as he thought about what he would do when they got back to their world.

The doors opened, Sydney snuggled up to him, and they entered. This time, they were ushered to the front to take their appropriate seats next to his parents. When they sat down, Jasani and Ayanna stood up in royal splendor. The room became silent.

"Finally, our son has returned home. Many of you know the struggle we faced in trying to find him. We never stopped looking." Jasani turned and looked at Lincoln. "It hurts my heart deeply that my...I mean, our son doesn't know who we are or how we stand by each other. Our family has been strong and has been fighters since we became our own nation. As the royal family of this nation, we have many responsibilities, and the main one is protecting our nation against anyone who wants to bring harm to us. This is something I will do until my last breath on this planet. And I hope my son will one day see that running this country is not a job but an honor." Ayanna nudged Jasani a little. "I guess that's my signal to stop." He laughed and took his seat.

Ayanna playfully rolled her eyes. She extended her hand to Lincoln, and he accepted it and held it. "My son, you don't know the joy and pleasure it brings me just looking into your beautiful face. I've dreamed of what you would look like since the day you were taken." She started to get emotional.

Tightening her grasp on his hand, she took a few moments to recompose herself. "I'm sorry, everybody, but you know he is my first-born, and I've talked about him every day since that dreadful day. I wish there was a way to go back in time so that I could protect my baby better so that I could have shared his growing moments. Just the mere fact that he made it back to us shows that he's a fighter. He's one of us. I don't care if people say otherwise, and if they do and I should hear them, they will face my wrath. Please stand and welcome my son and your future king, Prince Lincoln, and his wife, Princess Sydney."

The family around the ballroom stood up and clapped loudly while Sydney and Lincoln stared on. They'd felt bad beforehand, but they felt even worst about lying since the lie was now spreading.

The people clapped and cheered for about five minutes. Then Ayanna urged a reluctant Lincoln to stand and say a few words.

Lincoln cleared his throat and glanced around the room. "I want to thank everyone here for welcoming me and Sydney and my uncle Terrence. I know you all don't know my uncle Terrence, but he has been like a father to me ever since he found me years ago. And..." He paused as he stared at Sydney. "Sydney has been the woman who has protected me, laughed with me, and sometimes at me, but all the time loving me. I must admit that when we arrived, I didn't know what to think. Didn't know much about the country or my connection to it. In the very brief time that I have been here, I've seen care and love from my mother and father, and my sisters, too. It really breaks my heart that I didn't get to grow up experiencing that love with them. Not that my life was bad; it just would have been nice to know them all my life." Lincoln saw the servers standing at the back of the room. "The servers are looking at me, and I'm sure you all are hungry. I know I am. Thanks for everything, and I hope to meet all of you."

He took his seat, and the servers started serving the food.

***

Though breakfast had finished over two hours ago, the family and well-wishers kept coming up to greet Lincoln and Sydney and ask questions about everything from politics to how he was able to get back to Sea Islands. Uncle Terrence took the smart route and ran out of the ballroom before breakfast had even ended. Fearing that their stories wouldn't' match up, Sydney latched onto Lincoln and mostly let him explain and answer what people asked. When all the people in the line had left, Lincoln and Sydney were tired and happy that it was now over. As they walked out of the ballroom. Tia, Nicole, Ayanna, and Jasani came up to them.

"Don't you want to stay?" Nicole asked. "See all the love you got? These people already worship you like the second coming."

All the family members directed their gazes to Sydney and Lincoln.

"We will be back. That's a promise. We have to get back to work," Lincoln said, looking at Jasani.

"I'd love to see this job of yours. To give up being royalty is out-of-this-world insane," Tia said, still in disbelief that he was leaving.

"When will you be back?" Ayanna asked. "And I'm asking my new daughter."

Sydney was at a loss for words. She wanted to defer to Lincoln, but the question had been directed at her. "Very soon. Within the month. I will make sure we are back here."

Hearing her words, Lincoln turned to her.

"I like her. A woman with a strong mind. Maybe in that month, you will be back permanently to live?" Ayanna asked.

"Don't rush it, please," Lincoln said. "If Sydney says we are coming back, then I will be by her side."

Jasani checked his watch. "Thirty minutes until the introduction ceremony."

Leonard, the king's chief council, approached Jasani, whispered in his ear, and then left. Jasani looked at all of them.

"Everything okay?" Lincoln asked, seeing the concern on his father's face.

It took a second or two for Jasani to gather his thoughts. "I'm not sure. The American president is on the phone. Apparently, he wants to discuss a peace treaty."

"That's a good thing, right?"

Jasani took a deep breath and then chuckled as he breathed out. "With Americans, you never know. They are very deceptive people."

"Daddy, I'm sure Lincoln and Sydney know way more than we do about white people in America," Tia said.

"Yeah, we know a lot about how American white people operate," Lincoln said, laughing.

"I have to go, but I will see you all in thirty minutes." Jasani looked at Tia and Nicole. "Since you are already here, you two shouldn't be late." He then kissed Ayanna on the cheek and started to walk off. After about ten steps, he returned to the group. "Why don't you come with me?" he asked Lincoln.

Lincoln smiled. "Are you serious?"

"Son, I want you to come. America needs to see that I have a successor, the prince who will become king one day."

Lincoln wanted to remind his father that he was leaving tonight, but he stopped himself. "I'll come. Thanks."

Jasani turned and walked off, and Lincoln followed.

Tia, Nicole, and Ayanna focused their attention on Sydney.

"You have to tell us what Lincoln is really like," Nicole said, brushing up to Sydney.

"Yeah, were you the first and only girlfriend? How did you guys end up together? We need to know," Tia said. "And thirty minutes is enough time, so don't say that line."

"Calm down, Tia. Let her breathe," Ayanna said, protecting Sydney.

***

Jasani and Lincoln walked in his royal office and sat in front of the big TV screen on the wall as technicians wired them both up.

Jasani saw that Lincoln was nervous.

"This is nothing. Just another meet and greet."

"I thought this was about a peace treaty," Lincoln said, trying to figure out his father's angle.

"It is, but I need you to be my eyes and ears to notice what I might miss."

The technicians gave them the okay that the feed with the American President was now live. Lincoln inhaled and exhaled heavily. Jasani grabbed his hand to calm him down. The American president, Daniel McMillan, showed up on the screen. He had a strange expression on his face, as though he trying to figure out who Lincoln was.

"Hello, President McMillan. This is my son, Lincoln." Jasani turned and proudly looked at Lincoln.

Lincoln, not sure what to do, just waved at the screen.

President McMillan was perplexed. "King, did I miss something? I didn't think you had a son. I've only heard about your daughters all these years."

"My son was kidnapped almost twenty-five years ago while we were vacationing in Europe. We recently found him through a DNA test match."

President McMillan smiled. "This is a big surprise. I never knew you had a son who was kidnapped. Such a tragedy to hear. I'm so sorry for you and your family."

"It's good to have him back home."

"Do you want to postpone this meeting?" President McMillan asked, staring at Lincoln.

"No, my son needs to understand how to run our country and work with you and anyone else who may be president in the future."

"Lincoln, what is your background in politics?" President McMillan asked with a smirk on his face.

Jasani noticed the president's expression. "He will not be answering any questions today. Lincoln is only sitting in as an observer," he snapped.

"Oh, I'm sorry. Just wanted to get him up to speed."

"Don't take this the wrong way, but if my son needs any getting up to speed, I will be doing that."

"I understand."

"Good. So, are you going to remove your troops from our wall?" Jasani asked, holding in his anger.

"Our people want your people to rejoin the Union," President McMillan said. "There shouldn't be a wall separating our two countries."

"We're not rejoining a union when it serves no purpose for us to be a part of it. And the wall serves us perfectly. We control people crossing over into our country. We control our economy. We don't outsource our work. We train our people to be self-sufficient."

President McMillan's face turned bright red in anger. "We don't want to go to war to bring that wall down."

"Straight to war? Mr. President, you can't win. You have the numbers, but we have the power. Our resources far exceed what you have. Making threats like this does not help us find common ground. I just need you to remove your troops before we act. And my patience is thinning."

Lincoln sat there, nervous. He felt like he was stuck in the middle as President McMillan looked at them, thinking about his response.

"May God have mercy on you. This is not a war you can win, Jasani. Some of your allies will soon become our allies. I will crush you. When it is all said and done, you will be like the royal family in England, just another rich figurehead. The land you have will be returned to the United States of America. A hundred years from now, people will look back at Sea Islands like a myth. A small blurb in the history books about the king who couldn't. I will make it my mission to see that you are hated like President Lincoln. That's a promise."

"Why do you want to be let into our walls? Your people have tortured, raped, and killed my people for hundreds of years. Now that we are one of the most advanced countries and our economy is booming, you want to take what we have built. You are not being advised correctly, Daniel. If your troops aren't removed from our wall by morning, I will start action to have them removed. Not a threat, but a guarantee."

President McMillan's jaws tightened. "Let's sit down and discuss this at Camp David."

"Daniel, what would be the purpose of our meeting? You want into my country, and I'm not letting you. No need to meet about that. This continued discussion is a waste of your time and mine. It's fruitless."

"There has to be a way for us to work something out. The answer shouldn't be war," President McMillan said, as though the war was Jasani's idea.

Jasani chuckled. "Did I miss something? You were the one who brought up war."

"I just want to find a resolution to our common problem."

"We don't have a common problem." Jasani looked at his watch and saw that it was five minutes to noon. "We have to go. Have a great day, Mr. President."

"I would like for your royal council and my cabinet to discuss a treaty," President McMillan said, only agitating Jasani more.

Jasani looked at President McMillan with frustration and contempt. He didn't understand why the president wasn't getting the point. "Treaty for what?"

"Our government wants in. It's been reported that you have weapons of mass destruction."

"We do, and you do, too," Jasani said with a serious face as he glanced down at his watch again. "Have a nice day, Mr. President."

He had his technician cut the communication feed line, and the screen went black.

Lincoln sat there for a second, not sure which question in his head to ask Jasani first.

"I know you have a million questions; I will answer them after the introduction ceremony, okay?" Jasani got up and started to walk to the door. "We must not be late."

Lincoln quickly got up and followed him.

Chapter EIGHT

As people gathered on the front lawn of the castle for the introduction ceremony for Lincoln, there wasn't an empty space to be found. Introduction ceremonies were only for royal occasions, when announcing births, deaths, and power changes. The atmosphere was filled with joy since the last introduction ceremony had been over twenty-five years ago, when Tia and Nicole had been born.

Waiting for Jasani and Lincoln were Ayanna, Tia, Nicole, and Sydney. Terrence was sitting in a chair near the entrance. The lady foursome had spent the last twenty-five minutes together, and things seemed to be going well until Tia pulled out her phone and started taking pictures. Sydney did her best to avoid being in any of the pictures.

"Come on, sister-in-law. Just one picture," Tia asked. "You gonna make me beg."

"I'm not a big picture-taking person. I'm sorry," Sydney said, hiding behind Ayanna.

Ayanna looked at Tia. "Tia, leave her alone. It's okay for her to not be in the pictures. Not everyone wants to be on the internet."

"Sorry, I don't see what the big deal is with one picture. She's family now."

"Sydney, just take the one picture so she can move one, please," Nicole said, wanting them to stop all the picture-taking madness.

"Okay, one picture," Sydney said.

Ayanna turned to her. "You don't have to."

"One picture shouldn't hurt."

Sydney went over to Nicole and Tia, who gave her camera phone to Nicole.

"You not going to be in it?" Sydney asked Nicole.

"Please, Tia does way too much social media for me."

"Say cheese," Tia said with her arm wrapped around Sydney's neck. Before Sydney could react, the picture was taken.

Lincoln and Jasani came over and joined them. Tia looked at the picture and smiled. She then attached the photo and texted it to her friend Eric, with the message: "Find out who this is. Name Sydney Douglas. Police officer in Chicago. Need it pronto, like the fingerprints I sent earlier."

Jasani walked to the podium. He glanced around at the crowd of people on the lawn and at the many cameras pointing at him.

"Today is one of the proudest days of my life!" He paused and looked back at Lincoln. "My son is now home. He is once more with his people. For years, people would ask me, 'Why do you work so hard?' and I would say, 'For my son to one day come back and run this country.' I wanted to make sure that when he stepped into my footprints, they fit comfortably for him. I never wavered on his return. I knew he was out there somewhere and would find his way home. Our family had a hole in our hearts that was bigger than the Pacific Ocean if it was empty. But today our hearts, our

129

ocean, are filled with joy and happiness. We are one again. This day will forever be known as 'the Day of Hope,' and we will celebrate it today." Jasani looked at Lincoln. "Son, come here."

Lincoln turned to look at Sydney. He was so happy that he kissed her, surprising him and her. She kissed him back, and then he stepped up next to Jasani on the podium.

"Son, please face me," Jasani said, and Lincoln turned to him. "Now, take one knee."

Lincoln got down on one knee and glanced back at Sydney, both unsure of what was happening.

"I, King Jasani of Sea Islands, crown you, Lincoln Douglas, as Prince Lincoln, and that is how you will be addressed from this day forth. You will have all the rights of the royal family and the protection of the royal guard, and you will also be granted all the executive powers over the royal council that I have. And if I am incapacitated, retired, or meet my untimely demise, you will be crowned the king of Sea Islands without any question to your authority. Do you accept this honor?"

Lincoln froze. He also felt bamboozled by Jasani. He looked around the lawn and at the cameras; everyone was waiting for his response. But when he saw his mother's eyes upon him, he felt compelled to not let her down.

"I accept," he said, giving his father the evil eye.

Jasani smiled. He placed a small crown on Lincoln's head and then helped him to his feet and gave him a hug. "I love you, son." Jasani and Lincoln faced the crowd. "I present to you Prince Lincoln," Jasani said to cheers.

Lincoln, though dejected, mustered up a smile as his father presented him to the people. The rest of the family joined them.

***

In the Oval Office, President McMillan had just finished watching the introduction ceremony.

"Where the hell did this son come from? Disappeared and just popped back up after all these years?"

Four men walked into the office. Three were wearing navy suits, and one man was a four-star general.

"Mr. President, what is the plan?" the four-star general asked.

President McMillan looked at all four men. "Rip their hearts out. I want that wall down by the end of the week."

The general stared at the president with confidence. "Mr. President, I'll have it down in two days. They won't know what hit them."

All four men smiled at one another.

***

Later that afternoon, back in the bedroom, Sydney and Lincoln lay in each other's arms, naked. With her head on his chest, a lot of thoughts were running through her head. She just didn't know how to begin a discussion with him now that they had slept together. In the past, it had been easy to talk to him, but now that their hearts were connected, she didn't want to ruin things before they'd even started.

Lincoln could tell she had something on her mind. It surprised him that she wouldn't speak, since she was not one to be silent for this long. He kissed her on the head. "What are you thinking?"

She smiled. "Is this cheating or an affair?"

Lincoln bust his gut with laughter at the remark. "Well, cheating seems so dirty. I thinking cheating is just sex and cheap motels, whereas an affair is upscale, classy. You know, the two people might share a dinner and maybe a walk in the park before the event."

"The event? Is that what this is called?"

"The event has many different aliases," he said with a smirk.

"So, is this a cheating or an affair event?"

He looked at the vaulted ceiling and all the new furniture in the room. "This is definitely an affair. We're in a damn castle." He laughed. "And technically, it's neither. We are posing as husband and wife. I'm at a loss on what the rules are on cheating or affairs if you're in a different universe."

"Since you're Prince Lincoln, that makes me your princess."

He kissed her on the head again. "I like the way that sounds."

She frowned. "I guess it will be like Cinderella after the ball when we get back."

Though he couldn't see her face, the sad tone of her voice was a good indication of her feelings.

"I'm sorry if I have complicated things further. But I don't apologize about my feelings for you. This has been a huge weight lifted off my shoulders, mind, and heart. I know I'm nowhere near perfect and that when we get back, things will be different, but not my feelings or desire to be with you. I hope you understand that my intentions are to be with you in this universe and in any other one that we are in. I love you."

Sydney pulled herself up and faced him. She gazed into his eyes. "I love you, too. I know when we get back that you will need to resolve things before we can really move forward. I promise to wait on you through it all."

As they kissed, someone attempted to open the bedroom door. They grew silent, hoping the person would leave. The person then knocked.

"Open up. It's me, Terrence."

Sydney and Lincoln panicked. She jumped up, grabbed her clothes from the floor, and ran into the bathroom. Lincoln threw on his underwear, pants, and a t-shirt and went to answer the door. When he opened it, he blocked the doorway enough to prevent Terrence from walking in.

"What's up, Unc?"

Terrence peeked inside a little. "Where's Sydney?"

"Taking a shower. Why?"

"We need to get back home now!" Terrence said, almost like he was afraid to stay any longer than necessary.

"What you do?"

Terrence glanced away, not really wanting to tell him. "Okay, I called and talked to myself. It was weird. He's still a beat cop. Never been promoted. He's married, with two sons."

"I'm sure with Sea Islands as a country, racism in this world was probably worse than ours. I'm surprised you found yourself still living in Chicago."

"Me, too."

"Who did you tell him you were?"

"I told him I was his uncle Dennis from Philly, which happened to still be correct here, too."

"You shouldn't have made that call."

Terrence rolled his eyes. "Tell me something I don't know, genius."

"It's time for us to go home," Lincoln said, looking at the bathroom door. He didn't notice that it was cracked a little, that the shower wasn't running, or that Sydney was by the bathroom door, eavesdropping on their discussion.

About the same time, Dalilah approached Terrence from behind and, unbeknownst to him, listened in on their discussion, too.

"How is Sydney doing?" he asked. "Did something happen between the two of you?"

Lincoln gave him a weird scowl. "What do you mean by that?"

"Man, you are not five years old anymore. Did you and her sleep together? And you know what I mean by sleep."

133

Sydney smiled in anticipation of the answer Lincoln would give his uncle.

"No, no, definitely not happening. I'm still with Sonia. Me and Sydney are only friends."

Sydney became misty-eyed with sadness, and she sat on the toilet.

"Are we still leaving tonight?" Terrence asked. "If I stay longer, I'm going to Chicago."

"Yeah, that's not going to happen. We leave at 10 PM. I confirmed it with David an hour ago."

"What are you going to tell Sonia when we get back? I'm sure she will have lots of questions."

"Right now, I don't know what to say about any of this. This is foreign territory for me. Where would I even start?"

"I just hope that people aren't still trying to kill us," Terrence said with uncertainty. "I'm not sure I want to be shot again. I might not get the same treatment back in our world."

"We can't run forever."

"Are you sure you want to go back and live? You're a prince now. If you want to stay, then I'm with you."

"What about before, you saying you had to get back?" Lincoln said, giving Terrence the stink eye.

"That was before all this. This can be my retirement village. My nephew is the prince. You could probably make me a knight of the royal guard or court."

Sydney came storming out of the bathroom with attitude. "I'm ready to go."

Terrence looked at Lincoln, who looked at her with confusion on his face.

"Are you okay?" Lincoln asked.

"No, I'm fine. I know I have a lot to do when I get back home. I do have a life. This here is your world, not mine."

"Unc, I'll see you in an hour. David wants us to meet him in the back." Lincoln closed the door on Terrence's face before he could respond.

Dalilah saw the door close and quickly scattered off in the opposite direction from Terrence.

Lincoln went over to Sydney, but she took a step back. "I didn't mean what I said."

"You didn't say anything you didn't want to say. You had an opportunity to tell Terrence, and you couldn't. And that was Terrence. If I expected you to be truthful about us to anyone, it would have at least been him. And you couldn't."

"I love you, Sydney. You got to believe me."

"I know you love me. That's not the point. I don't want a love in the dark. Yes, I know you are with Sonia and say you plan on ending that, but are you really?"

Lincoln took a step forward and grabbed her hands. He pulled her to him. "Only an act of God is going to stop me from being with you. Sonia is a good person, so I don't take pride in ruining what we had. But I know it's your heart that I want beating next to mine for the rest of my life."

"We'll see," Sydney said as she brushed past him on her way out the bedroom door.

Lincoln thought about running after her, but he felt that it would only make things worse at this time. He figured that after he ended things with Sonia, he would go to Sydney with a clean slate for them to build their relationship on.

***

Dalilah made it outside without being seen. She called her father, King Tanana.

"Yes, my dear Dalilah, how are things going there in Sea Islands? Is the Prince what you expected?"

"I don't think this union is going to happen. He has a wife already and seems happy," she said, pouting.

"Many men of power, my dear, have two wives. The king promised me that you and he would unite our two kingdoms. If this is not the case, I will have to make other arrangements. What would you like me to do?"

There was silence for a few seconds.

"Don't agree to anything until after we are married. I think something weird is going on here."

"What do you mean?" her father asked with great interest.

"I'll find out more and give you a call tomorrow morning."

Her father looked down at a piece of paper titled; "A Declaration of War Against Sea Islands."

"Find out what you can, but I need to hear from you by midnight."

"Why so soon?" she asked.

"I will not be made a fool of. The king made a promise, and broken promises have grave consequences."

"Okay, Father, I'll talk to you soon."

"I will wait for your call, my dear, at midnight."

"Bye, Father," she said. As she hung up the phone, she wondered why her father wanted to move with such urgency.

***

Though the two leaders had been at a standstill during their meeting, the American military force was still on the other side of the Sea Islands' wall,

136

positioning themselves for imminent war. The Americans were planning a surprise attack before midnight. The troops were ready, with assault weapons, tear gas, hand grenades, and tanks, to storm the wall when the order came down. On the other side, the Sea Islands troops were operating like business as usual.

***

At ten o'clock sharp, the plane was ready for take-off when the SUV carrying Lincoln, Sydney, Terrence, Ayanna, and Jasani pulled up.

Little did anyone know, but Dalilah was already on the plane, hiding under the bed in the master suite. She knew something was up with them leaving at night after overhearing bits and pieces of Terrence and Lincoln's conversation. She wasn't sure where they were going, but she couldn't resist finding out.

When the SUV stopped, Terrence said his byes and quickly jumped out of the vehicle and ran onto the plane. Sydney and Lincoln, who hadn't spoken a word to each other since she'd left the bedroom upset, got out slowly. Ayanna and Jasani both had long faces, regretting the fact that their son was leaving them again. When the foursome reached the bottom steps of the plane, Ayanna embraced Lincoln with all the love in her body.

"Son, I wish you would stay," she said, weeping.

He saw her sadness and wished he could stay, but he knew that for him to move on with Sydney, he needed to end things back in Chicago first. And then maybe work on Sydney coming back with him. He did know that he wanted to come back and learn more about this universe, its people, and his family. What he didn't know was if he wanted to live there for the rest of his life.

"I'll be back. I promise you." He kissed her on the cheek.

137

Ayanna looked at Sydney and cried, "Make sure my baby comes back, okay?"

Sydney stared at Lincoln. "I will do everything possible for that to happen. You have my word," She hugged Ayanna and kissed her on the cheek.

Ayanna pulled out a gold clip from her hair and handed it to Sydney. "Take this. With this, you will always be close to me."

Sydney looked at it and smiled.

"Don't lose it," Ayanna said as she took it back and clipped it in Sydney's hair.

"Thank you," Sydney said after Ayanna was finished.

"It was a pleasure meeting you, Sydney," Jasani said. "I look forward to seeing the two of you back here real soon."

"Me, too," Sydney said as they embraced.

She left and boarded the plane while Ayanna went back and got into the SUV. Jasani and Lincoln stood there, looking at one another, searching for the right words to say. Jasani knew the dangers that Lincoln would face upon going back. He just wished Lincoln realized it.

"Son, are you sure you want to rush back this soon? Your mother and I would love for you all to stay longer. I'm still worried about your safety."

"I'll be okay. I need to go back and clear up some issues in my life. Just can't jump to another world and leave the old one a mess." Lincoln laughed.

"Oh, this is about Sonia," Jasani said. Lincoln was speechless. "Son, it's okay."

"How did you know?"

Jasani smirked. "I'm a very powerful man. I have information at my fingertips whenever I need it and wherever I need it from. When you popped up on the radar, we did a thorough check on you to make sure we knew everything. Couldn't afford a mistake. But I do know this. You don't want to lose that woman on the plane. That would be a big mistake. She loves you."

"Yeah, it's just not that easy," Lincoln said, imagining Sonia punching him in his face.

"It can be." Jasani handed Lincoln a phone.

"What's this for?" Lincoln asked.

"You can contact me on this no matter where you are."

Lincoln snickered. "So, all this time, I could have called back to Chicago?"

"No, the phone doesn't work like that. It must be paired with a phone in our world. It's like your satellite phone, but with a farther reach."

"Yeah, a universal reach."

"If something happens, just push one, and it comes directly to me," Jasani said with tears in his eyes. "I will have someone get you within the hour. It has a satellite locator as well."

"So, what are you going to do about the Americans at your wall?" Lincoln asked with grave concern.

Jasani took a deep breath. "In your history, blacks had something like a wall, but they were fooled into thinking that the white man was doing them a favor with the civil rights movement. That period ruined the black economy and destroyed their unity and pride. It turned black people against one another even further. I saw it as a kid with my father when he would take me to your world. I thought that when I went there to discuss our universe and share our technology, it would be a great thing for us all, but they just wanted the resources and to destroy us. I'm not letting that happen here."

"I'm glad I found you all. It's great to know I have family. Uncle Terrence did a wonderful job raising me, but it was just him and me."

"Not anymore, son."

Jasani hugged Lincoln. Lincoln didn't want to get into a crying fest, so he held back his tears.

"I better go," he said, pulling away and walking up the stairs to board the plane. He waved back at Jasani as the cabin door closed.

When Lincoln walked down the aisle to sit down, he looked at the door to the master suite, which was closed.

"Is someone back there?" he asked David as he passed by him.

"No, the door is closed because we are not using it. Unless you and the wife want to."

Lincoln looked over at Sydney and saw the scowl on her face. "No, I think we are good sitting out here."

"Well, it won't take us long. Buckle up." David got up and went to speak with the pilot.

Lincoln went down and stood over Sydney. "Is someone sitting here?" he asked playfully. Sydney turned her head away from, him ignoring his comedic gesture. Lincoln continued to walk down the aisle and sat next to Terrence.

Terrence smirked at him. "What the hell did you do to her? And don't say nothing."

Lincoln got up from his seat and moved further back to avoid answering the question.

As he buckled up, David returned and did the same. The plane jetted off into the night sky.

In the Situation Room at the White House, President McMillan and his top advisors were watching live events on the screen of their troops getting prepared for the invasion into Sea Islands.

"Are we a go, Mr. President?" one of his advisors asked.

"Let's initiate the battle," the president said sternly, looking around the room. "Operation Take Back in motion."

"General, it's a go. Engage," the secretary of defense said through the microphone on the table so that the military officers not in the room would begin the attack on the Sea Islands' wall.

On the screen, the tanks smashed through the wall, and the troops followed behind them, killing any Sea Islands soldiers in their path. The Sea Islands soldiers were totally surprised by the attack.

***

Tia was leaving an event downtown when she got a call from her friend Eric. She had sent him the picture of Sydney to research her background earlier.

"What you find out?" she asked.

"Does she have a twin sister with the same name?" Eric asked.

"I don't think so. Why?"

"Funniest thing is that there is a Sydney Douglas and Sydney Martin. Born the same day, the same year, the same everything, but one lives in Chicago as a police detective, and the other is a sheriff in Memphis, Tennessee. Sydney Douglas's information was just updated this week. I think something is fishy about her. I back-dated the system, and there was no record of a Sydney Douglas before yesterday."

"What about Lincoln Douglas?"

"Same with him. Until yesterday, the last record of him was almost twenty-five years ago, when he disappeared."

"He's an imposter!" she said, feeling like she had figured it out. "I knew something wasn't right about them."

"Hold on. He's the real deal. DNA, fingerprints, everything matches up. It's just he had no record for all those years until now."

"I'm getting to the truth. Thanks, Eric," Tia said as she hung up and dialed her father.

Still in the SUV, heading home after dropping off Lincoln and Sydney, Jasani answered the phone. "Hello."

"Dad, I think Lincoln and Sydney are not who they say they are. Don't trust them. They are probably working with the Americans."

Jasani got another call. "Hold on," he said as he clicked over to the other line. "Yes, what is it?"

It was the defense secretary. "The Americans have attacked our wall. Several of our troops are dead. How do you want to respond?"

Jasani was pissed. He couldn't believe that President McMillan had attacked him. "Initiate Operation Ether."

"Yes, King Jasani. I will engage now."

"Confirmed. Initiate Operation Ether," Jasani said, hanging up the phone. He didn't even bother with continuing the call with Tia.

Chapter NINE

The plane landed smoothly on a short landing strip behind an old, abandoned building about thirty miles south of Chicago. When the group exited the plane, two unmarked vehicles were waiting for them. Sydney, Lincoln, and Terrence got in one vehicle, while David and three of his men got in the second vehicle, parked behind.

When they got in the car, Sydney pulled out her phone and noticed that it was working again. She quickly called Casey. A group of agents at the Manteno State Hospital answered the call, but they stayed silent, waiting for the person on the other line to speak first.

"Hello? Hello? Casey, are you there? This is Sydney," she said. When no one replied, she hung up. "Something is wrong."

"What happened?" Terrence asked.

"Someone picked up the phone but didn't say anything. Casey doesn't let anyone use his phone."

"Yeah, that's right," Lincoln agreed.

He then called Sonia.

"Hello," she said.

"Hey, Sonia, it's me, Lincoln. Are you okay?"

Sydney rolled her eyes in his direction, knowing who he was talking to.

"Hey, Lincoln," Sonia said as a room filled with agents listened in on the conversation.

"I'm sorry about the other night and today. I didn't mean to ghost you like that."

"No problem. I'm just dealing with some issues at work. How did things go with your uncle?" Sonia asked nonchalantly.

He could hear the stress in her voice. "Are you alone?" he asked, sensing that she wasn't.

"Yeah, I'm alone. Who else would be at my place with me besides you? We do need to talk soon."

"We will. I still need to take care of something. I'll make it over there as soon as possible."

"Come now," she said. "How is Terrence?"

"Did anything happen? Did the cops contact you?"

The agents in the room were showing her pictures of her parents being tortured in the prison cell.

"Lincoln, I'm pregnant."

"What?" he said, glancing over at Sydney.

"I just found out today. That's why I'm at home. I don't know what I'm going to do. I need to see you...now, please."

"Okay, I'll be over in an hour."

"Where are you now?" she asked, reading the words from the piece of paper the agents had put in front of her face.

"Outside of Chicago. I'll be there soon. Don't worry."

"Okay. Hurry up. Bye." Sonia hung up.

When Lincoln got off the phone, Sydney and his uncle looked over at him with curiosity.

"How mad was she?" Terrence asked.

"Not mad at all. She was actually nice."

"What did she say?" Sydney asked.

Lincoln thought about telling the truth, but he knew that wasn't a good move right now with everything that had happened with Sydney.

"Just asking questions about where I was at and saying that she wanted to see me."

"So, are you going to see her?" Sydney asked, frowning. "I thought we were staying together until we knew things were safe?"

"I need to stop by her place first," Lincoln said, avoiding eye contact with Sydney.

"Nah, I'm going by the station to find out what's going on," Terrence said. "You can deal with that girlfriend mess on your own."

Sydney looked at her phone and then showed the two men what she'd seen. "Chief Clayborn and Walter are both dead. These two other guys died with them." She focused back on her phone and continued to read the news story.

Terrence looked at the pictures of the men. "Those are the guys who shot the woman at my house and me."

"None of this is making sense right now," Lincoln said. "Why would they be connected to this?"

"Maybe those two men killed Monty and Walter because of us?" Terrence said, running the thought in his mind.

"Doesn't add up to me," Lincoln said. "The chief and Uncle Walt don't know anything about this. But they do know your schedule and where you live."

"Monty did call me, asking when I was leaving the office."

145

"Maybe they are part of this," Lincoln said, trying to see how Monty and Walter fit into the puzzle.

In denial, Terrence wasn't buying his old friends having anything to do with him getting shot. "Nah, not them. They wouldn't sell me out. We go back like twenty-five years."

"Why wouldn't they?" Lincoln asked. "You always talking about Monty would do anything for money. You even said that at one time, you thought he might have been doing something illegal."

Terrence side-eyed him. "I would bet my life on that. They wouldn't hurt you or me."

Sydney finished reading the article. She exhaled and looked at Lincoln and Terrence. "I wouldn't make that bet yet. Walter and this guy here named John Thomas are half-brothers." She pointed at the man who had been going by the name of Sergio.

"Damn," Terrence said, deeply disappointed. "I don't want to believe it, but it does make sense. Monty and Walter's lifestyles were above their pay grades, even for the chief of police. Monty had courtside seats at the United Center and had a four-bedroom full-floor condo unit in the Waldorf Astoria over in the Gold Coast."

"Damn, that's over at least ten million," Sydney said.

"I still don't know the purpose. Was it all for the money? Kill us and get money?" Lincoln shook his head, saddened.

"Seems that way," Terrence said, staring off into space, steaming mad.

Sydney tried calling Casey once more and still got no answer. "I think something happened to Casey. I'm going to check on him, and then we can all meet back up at the precinct. Let's call it 7 AM. Is that okay? It's 1 AM right now."

146

"Perfect. It will give me time to rest," Terrence said, yawning. "I need to clear my head and figure this shit out."

Sydney glanced over at Lincoln. "What about you? Are you staying over at Sonia's?"

Sydney's question garnered the attention of Terrence, who listened closely, though he appeared to be looking out the window as the SUV drove down the interstate.

"That is not the plan," Lincoln said.

"Then what is the plan?" she replied with one eyebrow raised.

"Okay, I'm done with the games," Lincoln said, loud enough for Terrence and Sydney to hear. "I'm in love with you, Sydney. I'm going to talk to Sonia and see what is really going on, and then I'm coming back to your place. Is that okay?" he asked with a smile on his face.

Sydney beamed with joy as she removed her seat belt to kiss him. "I love you, Lincoln."

Terrence sat there, stunned, as he looked at them. "Excuse me, what the hell just happened?"

"She's the one, Unc."

Terrence laughed. "You finally figured that out."

Lincoln tapped on the separation window for the driver to open it.

"Hey, contact David in the other car. We need to split up. I'm going to jump in the car with him."

"Okay, Prince Lincoln," the driver said as he closed the window.

***

Back on the plane, Dalilah peeked her head out of the master suite. Seeing that it was empty, she quietly departed the plane. As she walked from the back of the warehouse to the front, she saw no one. She pulled out her phone and tried to make a call, but her phone didn't work. She grew infuriated with it, yelling at it every time nothing happened. "I hate technology!" After several minutes of not being able to make a call, she started walking out toward the main road, where she saw lights. Halfway down the road, a white truck driver in a semi pulled up to her.

"Hey, honey, you need a ride?" he asked.

"Where am I?" she asked with an air of conceit.

"Just outside of Chicago. Do you want a ride or not? You look like you're dressed for a ball," the trucker said with a laugh. "Just to let you know, Cinderella, not too many rides are coming this way this late at night."

"Chicago?"

The trucker smiled. "Yep, the Windy City."

Dalilah looked around and became spooked after realizing that she was alone in a strange environment. "Can you take me downtown?"

"Where downtown?"

"Anywhere. I will be able to find my husband once I'm there. My phone died on me," Dalilah said with a grin, showing her dimples.

The trucker was disappointed at the mention of a husband. He started to pull off and just leave her, but he had a change of heart when she took off her watch and threw it at him.

"I don't have money, but you can have that," she said, waiting for him to respond.

The trucker examined the watch. He knew it was real gold. "Where did you get this from?"

"Kenya. We have so much gold. Are you going to give me the ride?"

The trucker opened the passenger door and extended his hand to help her up. She got in. He looked at her attire and the diamond earrings and necklace.

"Who are you?"

"I'm Princess Dalilah from Kenya."

148

The trucker smiled at her, assuming she was lying. "I'm the king of trucking, but you can just call me Sam," he said as he started his truck up.

"Do you have some money I can borrow? I forgot my money."

He reached into his shirt pocket and handed her a wad of cash. "That's three hundred dollars."

She took the money. "Thank you," she said as she and faced forward, watching Sam from the corner of her eye.

***

"Midway Airport just reported a strange object that popped up on the radar and then disappeared. That's them. They are back. I know it's them," Agent Jones said to her team.

Sonia sat nervously while the agents talked strategy amongst themselves. She didn't want Lincoln to come, but she knew that if he didn't, her family might be dead.

Agent Jones walked over to her and sat down in front of her. "I know you hate this, but you are helping your country out. This is about our national security."

Sonia refused to look at her. "This is what people do in terrorist countries. My family didn't do anything to anyone. And Lincoln isn't some alien from another planet. This is ridiculous. I can't believe this is how our government wastes taxpayer money."

Agent Jones took a deep breath and then exhaled. "You think you're right?"

"I know I'm right. I know him."

"Okay, this is what we are going to do. I'm going to let you prove to me that he's innocent. Is that fair?"

Sonia slit her eyes at the agent with skepticism. "What's the catch?"

"No catch. I will have my agents hide outside, and we will let you talk to him. If he lies about the plane ride, then we will bust in and arrest him. And if he doesn't, I will testify in court that he is not involved. Is that fair?"

Sonia contemplated the offer. Since she was convinced that Lincoln was innocent, she didn't see anything she had to lose. "Okay. And your agents are going to be outside?"

"Out of plain sight. We will still have to take him downtown to complete the official report."

"Is there another option?" Sonia asked.

"Yeah, we attack him right when he walks through those doors. And if he attempts to run, we shoot him immediately." Agent Jones glanced at her watch. "The clock is ticking. What is it going to be?"

"I'll talk to him. You'll see this is a big misunderstanding."

"Good choice." Agent Jones looked at the other agents. "Clear out of here. Let's quickly set up outside. Set up cameras and microphones. I want to make sure I have eyes and ears throughout this house."

***

"Pull over right here," Lincoln said to the driver.

The driver pulled the car into the parking lot of a CVS drugstore down the street. He cut off the lights and parked on the side where it was the darkest and they could barely be seen. David and two royal council guards were getting their weapons ready.

"I'm going in alone," Lincoln said. "If it's a trap, then at least I know you can get me out."

"Are sure you want to do this by yourself?" David asked.

"It's about a mile away. If there are police there waiting on me, I want to see them before they see me." Lincoln handed David the phone Jasani had given him.

David looked at it, not understanding why Lincoln was giving it to him. "You need this."

"If I'm not back in two hours, come get me. I don't want them capturing me and using this phone for their own purposes."

"I think you should take it with you for safety." David handed the phone back to Lincoln. "Just push one if something happens. Your father will notify me. I will push seven-seven-three for RED, and an aerial team will get you out of here."

"Okay," Lincoln said as he got out of the car.

***

The other car pulled up about two blocks away from Casey's house. Sydney took a gun from one of David's royal council guards.

"You be careful," Terrence said.

"You be careful down at the precinct," she replied. "I read the story about the chief and Walter's murder, but they didn't mention any leads or people of interest they are looking for. That's odd."

"Probably don't want to alert the person who did it," Terrence said with a shrug.

"Maybe that person is people, and it's us." Sydney pointed to them both. "Shit, I'm having a bad feeling about it all. I think Lincoln is going into a trap." She pulled out her phone and called him.

Lincoln answered. "Sydney, what's going on?" he asked as he approached the front door of Sonia's house.

"I think it's a trap! Get out of there now!" she yelled into the phone.

Static on the line distorted her words. "I can't hear you," he said.

"Get out!" she said at the top of her lungs, but again, he didn't understand what she was saying.

"I'll call when I leave Sonia's. It's going to be okay. Love you." He hung up the phone.

"Damn!" Sydney said to Terrence. "He couldn't hear me."

"Maybe it's not a trap."

Sydney shook her head in disgust. "My gut tells me it is. I should have gone to back him up."

"Don't worry about Sonia. He wants to be with you."

"It's not about her. Think about it. The chief and Walter was murdered, but nobody called our phones from the police. That would never happen. I get not calling you, since you did get shot, but I should have been contacted."

"You right about that! Damn, contact David!" Terrence said to the driver.

Just then, the driver and his partner were both shot in the head.

Bullets were flying everywhere as Terrence and Sydney tried to see where the shooters were coming from. Sydney got out of the car and made it to the driver. She pulled him out and jumped in his seat. She ducked down and was able to drive off without getting her, Terrence, and the royal council guard shot.

***

Sonia opened the door and smiled at Lincoln. She hugged and kissed him and then moved out the way so that he could come inside. He cautiously entered, looking around the place to see if someone was hiding. He kept a close eye on Sonia, especially with her acting all cool, like nothing was wrong.

"Why didn't you tell me Chief Clayborn and Walter were murdered?" he asked. "That would have been important to know."

"I had other things on my mind. Sorry." She sat down at the kitchen table. "How did you get here, anyway?"

"I got dropped off." He sat down across from her. "I need to talk to you about my parents, but I want to discuss you being pregnant first."

Agent Jones, who was outside the house, waiting to storm in, stopped in her tracks when he said that. "Check any car waiting a mile out in all directions leading to this house. His ride is still here," she whispered into the walkie-talkie.

"What about your parents?" Sonia said. "I thought they were dead."

"That's secondary to you and the baby. I'm not going to be an absent father."

Sonia tilted her head as she looked at him. "What are you saying, Lincoln?"

He paused. "Nothing. I just want to make sure I'm not like my parents."

"So, where did you go?" Sonia said, a concerned expression on her face.

"I never said I went anywhere," he replied.

"You went all disappearing act on me yesterday. After the hospital, I didn't know what to think. I thought something happened to you. I went to your uncle's house, Sydney's, and Casey's and couldn't find any of you guys. How do you think that made me feel? I want to be a part of your life."

"You are a part of my life," Lincoln said. "But I need to talk to you about us moving forward."

"Exactly. I'm going to be the mother of your child, and I don't know anything. Let me in, Lincoln."

"What do you want to know?"

"Tell me about your parents."

He smiled. "This is going to be weird, but you have to believe me."

"This isn't about some alien shit, right?"

"What are you talking about?" Lincoln knew that Sonia knew more than she was letting on.

"Nothing, just playing around," she said, hoping to cover up her slip-up.

Lincoln felt something was off. He thought about Sydney's call before he'd walked in and what she had been trying to tell him. "Hey, I need to use your restroom. Be right back." He walked into the bathroom and turned on the sink faucet. He pulled out his personal cell phone and the phone his father had given him. He called Sydney. The phone rang about three times, and he was about to hang up when she answered.

"Lincoln," she said as she erratically raced down the street, chased by police and other unmarked vehicles and time trying not to be shot.

He could hear all the background noise and shooting. "What's going on?"

"It's a trap! Get out of there!" she screamed into the phone.

He looked out the window, wanting to jump out of it. In the bushes, he saw some dark spots that looked like people on the ground. Then his gaze shifted around the bathroom, and he saw the camera in the corner, pointed directly at him. "Damn, it's too late."

"I'm coming for you," Sydney said as she turned down another street.

"Just get to safety. I'll be okay," Lincoln said, taking deep breaths. "Is Uncle Terrence still with you?"

"Yeah, but he's bleeding."

"What? He got shot again? No! Sydney, I love you. Just get to safety and get him some help. I'll get out of this."

154

Terrence moved the dead guard out the way. He tapped Sydney on the shoulder and put his hand out for her to hand him the phone. She gave it to him.

"Lincoln," he said, breathing heavily and bleeding just as much.

"Unc, you okay?" Lincoln asked, grimacing at how his uncle sounded. He knew from his voice that unless he got medical assistance soon, he wasn't going to make it.

"Listen to me. Shut up for a second. Take the money I got and give it to me in your world. You got to leave here."

"Don't die on me, Unc!" Lincoln cried.

Terrence coughed up some blood. "I'm not sure how much time I had anyways. I should have told you that I have dementia."

"It doesn't matter now. I just don't want you to die. Hold on," Lincoln said, but then the phone went dead.

Sonia knocked on the bathroom door. "Is everything okay?"

Lincoln grabbed the phone his father had given him and pushed the number one. He turned his back to block the camera on the wall and broke the phone in half. He then placed the phone in the trash. He opened up the bathroom door. Sonia stood there, staring at him.

"Were you on the phone?" she asked suspiciously.

He stared at her, wondering if she had heard him. He assumed she had. "My uncle called me, asking if I had his car keys."

"That was that bitch Sydney, wasn't it?"

He didn't respond.

"What the hell does she want from you this late at night? Does she know what's going on?"

"Who's here? Come out," he said, looking around the room and out the window.

"What are you talking about?" Sonia asked, trying to act like everything was normal. "No one is here but me."

Agent Jones and three other agents came in the room from behind Lincoln.

"Liar." Lincoln turned around to face Agent Jones. "Did you enjoy the show?" he said, shaking his head.

"Cuff him. He's going with us," Agent Jones said. Then, to Sonia, she added, "You did a good job."

Sonia spit in her face. "Lincoln, she's lying. They were going to kill my parents."

"Are you pregnant?" he asked her.

She stood there, stewing, as she stared at Agent Jones. "No."

"You got me," he said as the agents handcuffed him.

Agents Jones stood face to face with him. "Do you want to tell me about the plane ride now, or is this something you wish to hold near and dear to your heart? I do have a way to break hearts."

"Lincoln, just tell her what you know. I know it's all Sydney."

Lincoln looked at Sonia with disgust. He wanted her to shut her mouth. "Sydney doesn't have anything to do with this."

"I'll be the judge of that. Your friend Casey definitely didn't break. That's a great friend choice. I got to give him credit. Oops, yeah, she was with Casey, too."

"Is he alive?" Lincoln asked, trying to break free of the cuffs.

"Get him out of here," Agent Jones said, punching him in the stomach to calm him down.

***

Jasani, Ayanna, Tia, and Nicole were in the Royal Family Protection Bunker safe room when Jasani's universal tech phone buzzed, alerting him that Lincoln was in danger.

He grabbed the phone quickly, hoping that Ayanna wouldn't notice since she was the only other person who knew about their parallel universal travels. It was too late. Ayanna heard and saw which phone it was. She went over to him as he pushed the number two on the phone dialer.

"Is that Lincoln?" she asked with intense nervousness.

Jasani didn't want to answer, but he knew that if he didn't say anything, her worrying would get even worse.

"Yes, but it will okay. I just alerted David so that he brings him directly back here."

"What about the war going on at our border? Will they make it past the American forces on re-entry?"

"I don't know," Jasani said, stretching his neck.

"We need to know," she begged. "I can't lose him again. Not like this. Can't our allies help?"

"I think Africa has turned against us. I have reached out several times but have not gotten a response."

"Because of Dalilah?"

"I think she told her father something bad. I'm not sure what."

"What happened to her, anyway? I haven't seen her since after dinner last night. I had the guards check her living quarters, and her things were there. God knows this could turn ugly for us if something bad happens to her."

Jasani's head fell on his desk in frustration. "We have to find her."

"Can we win without them?" Ayanna asked with a fearful look on her face.

Jasani exhaled. "I don't know, but we also can't allow them to join the American forces. That would crush us."

***

David and the driver were outside the car, smoking cigarettes, when his phone buzzed, letting him know that Lincoln was in trouble. David heard it and opened up the car door to grab it. As he reached for his phone, he and the driver were both attacked by Agent Mitchell and some of his agents. David couldn't believe that he had been caught. As they were escorting them to the back of their cars in handcuffs, he couldn't take his eyes off the backseat door, where his phone was. But when he saw the agent open the door and grab his phone, he became sick to his stomach.

***

At about 2:30 AM, the truck driver who picked up Dalilah dropped her off at the Chicago Police Headquarters on South Michigan Avenue.

As Dalilah slowly got out of the truck, she took in her foreign surroundings with fear.

"Is this safe?" she asked, glancing back at the truck driver.

"Honey, this is the police station. I don't think you will find a better drop-off location. Just go inside and tell them about your friends and man, and they will take care of you."

She scratched her head, closed the truck door, and said through the open window, "Thank you."

The trucker held up the gold watch. "No, thank you," he replied, and then he drove off.

Dalilah stood outside the station for a few moments, contemplating what she was going to say once she entered. After seeing some seedy individuals pass by, she hurried inside. She went straight to the counter, where a female police officer was staring at her computer screen and trying not to fall asleep.

"Hello," Dalilah said, startling the officer.

"Yes, may I help you?" the officer asked. She noticed what Dalilah was wearing. "Did a John stiff you, or were you attacked?"

Dalilah looked at her with confusion. "What is a John?"

"Are you from Chicago or lost?" The officer saw that something wasn't right with Dalilah.

"I'm from Kenya. I'm Princess Dalilah."

The officer smiled at her. "Yes, me, too. I'm royalty as well. All of us royals wander the night. What can I help you with?"

"I'm looking for Prince Lincoln. I just need to find him, and then I will be able to go back home with him."

A male officer behind the counter came up to the female officer. He whispered in her ear, "Is everything okay?"

The female officer laughed. "We are just having a royal conversation at three in the morning. I think she has been drinking a little too much," she whispered back.

"Is there someone else I may speak with to find Prince Lincoln?" Dalilah asked, looking around the precinct floor.

"No, I'm the one. Does this Prince Lincoln have a last name?"

"Yes, his name is Prince Lincoln Douglas of Sea Islands."

"Lincoln Douglas?" the female officer asked for clarity.

Dalilah smiled. "You know him?"

The female officer looked at the male officer. "She's looking for Lincoln Douglas."

Within a matter of seconds, the front door locked, and several officers emerged from the back.

Dalilah saw the reaction and thought it was strange. "Is something wrong?"

"No. Please take a seat right over there. A few officers will gladly help you find Lincoln Douglas."

Chapter TEN

It took great driving skills for Sydney to shake the people chasing them. She made it to Waterfall Glen Forest Preserve at 3 AM. She parked the car in the bushes and took Terrence out of the car. He was shot up badly and barely holding on.

"Save yourself," he said to her, seeing the tears in her eyes.

"No, Lincoln needs you."

"No, Lincoln has you now. You can save him."

Sydney threw his right arm over her shoulder. "You better not die on me."

She started walking into the forest, dragging him along. She'd carried him almost two miles when she stopped to take a break. She leaned him up against an oak tree.

"I can't go any further," he said. As he breathed heavily, blood flowed out of his body, and he became cold.

"You got to keep going!" she cried.

"We shouldn't have left that world. What were we thinking? Lincoln is now one of the richest people in the world, and we left that for this." He struggled to laugh. "You got to get him and leave this place. Don't come back. You will be queen one day. Queen Sydney, I like that."

She looked over at him, knowing that the end was near. It was hard watching her mentor and friend die in front of her, but she mustered up enough strength and went to his side. "I love you, Terrence. You are like a second father to me. I don't want you to die."

"As long as you and Lincoln live, I will never die," he said with a smile, and then his eyes closed.

She checked his pulse and didn't feel one. She fell to the ground, crying, next to his cold body.

***

Back in the underground basement at the abandoned Manteno State Hospital, about ninety miles from downtown Chicago, Lincoln was being waterboarded by Agent Jones. It angered and amazed her that he would not break after two straight hours of torture.

"Are you willing to die?" she asked him.

"I didn't do anything," he defiantly replied.

"You will never see the light of day again unless you talk to me first. I have video footage of this supersonic plane that you were on. We got you getting on and it disappearing into thin air. I want to help, but you don't seem to want to help yourself. So, we gonna play a little game. Since you're player one, we need another player. Come on out, player two."

The light came on in the room across from Lincoln, and right before his eyes, Casey appeared. Casey looked half-dead and out of it. He was strapped into a chair, and standing over him was a person in a protective rubber suit.

"He doesn't know anything," Lincoln said, trying to get her to let him go. "That's an innocent man."

162

"If he doesn't, then who does? And that is the first question of the game, Mr. Douglas," Agent Jones said with a smirk.

Lincoln looked over at Casey. "Okay, we got on a regular plane and took a trip to Florida. That's the truth."

Agent Jones paused to think about this. "Wrong answer."

The person in the rubber suit pulled out a machete and sliced Casey's right arm off. Upon seeing it, Lincoln vomited out his guts. The rubber-suit person then took a hot metal plate and used it to stop the bleeding. Casey was so drugged up that he didn't feel anything; he just stared at Lincoln with no expression.

"You have to stop this. I'm begging you," Lincoln said, in tears.

"Where is the plane that brought you back?" Agent Jones pressed. "I'm not stopping until I get some answers."

Lincoln looked over at Casey. "I promise you; I don't know."

Agent Jones dropped her head, mad at his answer. "Do you even care about your friend?"

Lincoln simmered.

"Well, the game is about to get even more interesting. I found another friend."

"Just let her go," Lincoln said, thinking the person was Sydney.

"Oh, that girlfriend is quite crafty. But I will find her, too. No, I have your getaway driver. As they say, smoking will eventually kill you."

Lincoln looked to his right and saw David strapped up to a chair, just like Casey.

"I don't know him," Lincoln said.

"That's very funny since he's at the top of my list of strange things right now." Agent Jones pulled out her iPad and showed Lincoln a video of David's look-alike sitting in a police station. "You notice anything funny about that?"

"No. Like I said, I don't know him."

Agent Jones laughed. "That's what the guy in the live video feed is saying, too. It's very funny how these two men share all the same DNA."

"So, what if they are twins? I don't know him."

"I thought you might say that, but when my chief scientist checked their fingerprints, they were exactly the same. That's how I know that is not his twin. That's him, but an identical, out-of-this-world double of him."

"What are you saying?" Lincoln asked, looking at David and Casey.

"I think you know exactly what I'm saying. It's time for the games to end, Mr. Douglas. Where the fuck did you go?"

"Let Casey go, and I'll tell you everything."

Agent Jones looked over at Casey. "You heard the man. He said let him go."

The person in the rubber suit shot Casey in the head, killing him. Lincoln couldn't believe his eyes, that she had just had his best friend killed in front of him. He tried to get loose from the chains but couldn't.

Agent Jones laughed at his attempts. "This is no game, Lincoln. I want to know the truth about the plane and where you went."

***

In the American Situation Room, President McMillan was speaking to King Tanana through a live video feed.

"I'm still waiting on your response, King," President McMillan said. "We need your resources. Like I said, you will get Cuba and Puerto Rico."

"My daughter is still in Sea Islands. I need her alive," the king said, "before I make them my enemy."

"Where is she now?" President McMillan asked, annoyed by the king's hesitation.

164

"I don't know. She was supposed to contact me hours ago. I think something might have happened to her."

"Then this is the only way at this point. I don't want to say this, but King Jasani might have jumped the gun and killed her."

"Why would he do that?" King Tanana asked. "Unless your people leaked that we were in talks."

"My people didn't say a word. You have my promise. I just need you to give me your resources so that I can end King Jasani's tyranny."

"I will respond in about two hours. I want to give my daughter more time to contact me."

"We can't wait any longer. Their forces are starting to push us backward. I didn't know he had the wall filled with gasoline gutters. I've lost a lot of men. He needs to pay for that."

"My daughter is my top priority. You either wait or you don't; that's not my concern. Bye, Mr. President." King Tanana cut off the feed.

"Damn nigger!" President McMillan said in front of his advisors. "I don't care what you have to do, I need an edge in this war. This has to end quickly. We don't have the resources or manpower to win against them."

***

Sydney sat on the edge of the Des Plaines River, near the waterfall. She was scared, tired, and hungry.

"Lincoln, where are you?" she asked the night sky. "I got to find you. I know exactly where to start."

***

Back in the basement of Manteno State Hospital, Lincoln was crying uncontrollably about the death of Casey.

165

Agent Jones looked at him. "You should feel guilty. This is all your fault. If you would just tell me what I want, then everyone else will go home, except for him in the other room. I won't even go hunt down your girlfriend."

"I—" Lincoln started to say, but Agent Jones cut him off.

"Hold on, we now have another contestant." She gave him a wicked smile.

Lincoln's eyes popped out of their sockets as he looked around into the other rooms, trying to see who she could be talking about. Then he saw the person in the room to his left was Dalilah.

"No," he said, hoping to spare her to. "Let her go."

"Funny thing is, I don't need your twinster over there for now." Agent Jones pointed at David. "This one." She pointed at Dalilah. "This one doesn't have a problem telling me what I want. Chatterbox. Want to listen in?" Agent Jones turned on the switch on the wall.

"Yeah, my father is the king of Kenya. I'm a princess. The flight here was very fast. I have never been to Chicago, but judging from the map, it should take us longer than two hours from Sea Islands."

"What is Sea Islands?" the agent in the room with her asked. Lincoln gritted his teeth, knowing that there was nothing he could do to stop her.

"It's a country, one of the wealthiest in the world. My family and Lincoln's family have been connected for, I think, over a hundred years or so. I just came to Sea Islands. This was my first trip. My father wanted me to meet Lincoln before we got married. Our union is necessary for peace between our nations."

"How do you know Lincoln Douglas?" the agent asked.

"He's my match. I don't know much about him, but I know that he was abducted years ago and just recently reappeared in Sea Islands."

"Where is this plane that you came in on?"

166

Dalilah looked at the glass window, but she couldn't see anything in the room next door. "That would be hard to get back to. I do remember the truck driver that gave me a ride and the name on the side of his truck. Lucky Duck Trucks. His name was Sam."

Agent Jones looked at Lincoln with a devilish grin. "I got it, and I didn't even need to break your heart. You are lucky that I still need you."

Agent Jones left the room and met her other agents in the hallway. "Find out where she got picked up, and let's get extra people ready just in case it's a trap," she said. "I want to be ready for what might be there."

As the agents ran off, Agent Mitchell walked over to her. "Is this really happening? Aliens from another world?"

"I always knew there was something beyond those stars," she said, looking back into the room where Lincoln sat.

"What do you want to do about the other guy in the room?" Agent Mitchell asked.

"Leave him there. Put extra chains on him and lock the door. I don't know anything about these people. Lincoln and the girl are coming with us."

Agent Jones got a message on her phone. She looked back at Lincoln. "Hey, Lincoln, more bad news. Your uncle Terrence was found dead. Only the girl left. The other one turned on you very quick. I'll break this one, too, eventually."

Upon hearing the news, Lincoln tried his hardest to break free and get to Agent Jones.

"I'm going to make you suffer if I get out of here. You better kill me now," he said with vengeance in his voice.

As dawn broke, Jasani and Ayanna emerged from their safe room. Tia and Nicole were still asleep. The couple slowly walked up the stairs and onto the first floor.

"It's very quiet," Ayanna said, feeling a bit uneasy.

"Maybe you should go back down with the girls," Jasani said. He went over to the bookcase and grabbed a gun from one of the books.

"Okay," Ayanna said, and she made her way back to the safe room downstairs. As she got to the door that led downstairs, she saw several men heading toward her husband. "Jasani, run!" she yelled.

Jasani turned to run back to her, but the men jumped on him before he could take another step. One of the men attempted to get to Ayanna, but she closed and locked it before he could re-open it. Jasani's men came into the castle and tried to help, but the men who had snatched Jasani were able to slip away.

When Ayanna made it back to the safe room, Nicole was up. She met her mother at the door.

"Where is Daddy at?" she asked in a panic.

Tears filled Ayanna's eyes. "He's been captured. I got to get him back."

"What about our allies?" Nicole asked.

"Dalilah has gone missing. I have no clue where she might have gone," Ayanna said. "Her father refuses to help us."

Nicole huffed. "That's easy. Wherever Lincoln went, I'm sure she's not too far behind."

Ayanna froze, thinking about what Nicole had just said. That was the worst thing she could imagine with respect to Dalilah's whereabouts.

Nicole saw her mother's face turn pale. "Are you okay, Mom?"

Ayanna went and took a seat on the couch.

"Mom, where did Lincoln go, anyway? Shouldn't he be here?"

***

In the Situation Room, President McMillan waited for King Tanana to join the video call. When King Tanana joined, he saw that President McMillan was all smiles.

"Yes, Mr. President," King Tanana said as if he were annoyed. "I told you I would contact you once I located my daughter."

"No need. I got exactly what I needed without your help."

"What are you talking about?" King Tanana said, very concerned.

President McMillan chuckled. "I thought that might pique your interest a bit. But my operatives have gotten the big fish."

"What is this big fish?"

"I got King Jasani. He's on his way to Washington, D.C., as we speak. I no longer need your services or partnership. I will remember this moment, when I reached out to one of my enemies and got slapped in the face. You will pay for this in the future now that Sea Islands is mine."

***

The sun was now rising into the sky. With Dalilah's help, the agents had been able to track down Sam and obtain the location of the plane. The pilot was by himself, waiting for David to return. Agents Jones and Mitchell had their team strategically surround the plane. Agent Jones made sure to keep Dalilah in the dark as to what was really going on by keeping Lincoln and her apart from each other. As far as Dalilah knew, at this point, Agent Jones was helping her get back home.

Lincoln was being kept in the white van behind the car Dalilah was in, gagged and handcuffed. Agent Jones didn't want to take any chances of him escaping and ruining what she assumed was going to be a big discovery.

169

"So, what is our play?" Agent Mitchell asked her.

She studied the plane; she knew the risk of the pilot disappearing into the sky. She glanced back at the white van.

"Get him out of the van. He's going to be the bait. I need that pilot out of the cockpit."

She went over to Lincoln as the agents got him out of the van. He wasn't sure what was going on.

"Before I take this gag off of you and unhandcuff you, we need to have an understanding. If you scream or try to run, I promise you little Ms. Talkalot will be shot in the head. And that will be on you, Lincoln. And when I find that Sydney, I'm going to make sure you are front and center."

Lincoln nodded his understanding. Agent Jones had the men unhandcuff and ungag him. Lincoln looked around. He wanted to make a run for it into the woods.

Agent Jones saw his gaze shift to the woods. "You wouldn't get far, Lincoln." When he looked back at her, she continued. "I need you to go over to the nose of the plane and get the pilot to open it. That's a very simple request. Can you handle that?"

Lincoln nodded.

Agent Mitchell pulled Dalilah out of the car. Dalilah saw Lincoln and started to run to him, but the agent grabbed her by the hair and dropped her to the ground. He then put his gun to her head.

"One scream or movement and this will be the end of your story," he said.

Dalilah didn't understand what was going on. "My father is one of the wealthiest men in the world. If it's money, I can give it to you."

"Just shut your trap!" he said to her as he pressed the gun's barrel into her temple. Dalilah stopped all movement. She saw that this wasn't about money.

"What did he do?" she asked, looking in Lincoln's direction. "I'm not with him. I just want to go home."

"I thought you were to be wed to him, the prince? Now you jumping ship." Agent Mitchell laughed. "Typical woman."

Lincoln slowly walked to the nose of the plane. When he got there, he waved to get the pilot's attention, but the pilot was sleeping. Lincoln grabbed a rock and threw it at the window. The pilot woke up in a panic, and he looked down and saw Lincoln standing there. Lincoln pointed at the cabin door. The pilot got up and opened it. Immediately, agents rushed in and subdued him.

Agents Jones and Mitchell entered the plane, along with Dalilah and Lincoln, who were both handcuffed and gagged. The pilot soon joined them, and the agents threw him, Dalilah, and Lincoln into seats and directed their guns at them.

Four other agents quickly went through the plane, checking to see if anyone else was aboard. Once they saw that no one was there, they exited the plane and started to check the outside.

Agent Jones pulled the gag from the pilot's mouth. "Where are you from?" she asked.

"Autopilot!" the pilot screamed.

Everyone looked at him oddly until the plane's cabin door and hatches all closed automatically. Agents Jones and Mitchell scrambled to see what was happening and tried to reopen the doors. Even the cockpit door locked.

Agent Jones put her gun to the head of the pilot. "Stop this plane now!"

"Once autopilot is started, I can't stop it," he said. "It won't stop until we land in Sea Islands."

"I'm going to shoot you if you don't stop this plane now," she demanded.

The pilot scoffed. "There's nothing I can do. This is our protocol."

Agent Mitchell came over and punched the pilot in the face. He assumed brute force might get the pilot to change his mind. The plane rose up from the ground, into the sky.

"Land this plane now," Agent Mitchell demanded with fear on his face.

The bloody pilot looked at the two agents. "We will land in Sea Islands very soon."

Out of disgust, Agent Jones shot the pilot in the head.

"Why did you shoot him?" Agent Mitchell asked her angrily. "That's the pilot. You don't shoot the fuckin' pilot."

"He wasn't going to help us!" she yelled back at him.

"Now what? We have no idea what we are going into." Agent Mitchell took a seat.

Agent Jones went to Lincoln and pulled his gag off. "Where are we going?"

"Sea Islands. This is what you wanted, right?" he said sarcastically.

She pulled her gun out and pointed it at his forehead.

Lincoln smiled at her. "That wouldn't be in your best interest at all. I'm the best bargaining chip you got to make it back home. If I die, nobody will help you."

Agent Jones realized that he was right. She put her gun down and sat next to him. "You have to save us," she said with tears in her eyes.

Lincoln looked at her like she had lost her mind. "You murdered my best friend, and now you want me to save you?"

Chapter ELEVEN

Sydney snuck into Sonia's house from a window in the garage. She didn't know what to expect, since the last time she had talked to Lincoln, he had been there in what they'd assumed was a trap.

As she walked around the house, she thought she was doing a good job of not making a sound. But when, from out of nowhere, Sonia jumped on her and knocked her out, she realized that wasn't the case.

Sonia dragged Sydney down to the basement and tied her up. When Sydney woke up, she was confronted by an angry Sonia, who repeatedly slapped her.

"Why don't you just leave my man alone," Sonia said, staring at her.

Sydney struggled to get loose, but couldn't. "I'm going to kill you."

"You know, I tolerated you for all these years, but now I actually have the government on my side if I decide to kill you right here in my basement. I'll be a hero."

Sydney saw the seriousness in the threat. "Sonia, I'm not your enemy."

Sonia laughed. "If you're not my enemy, then I definitely don't know shit. I hate you, and you hate me."

"I don't hate you," Sydney said, hoping to ease the tension a bit.

Sonia grabbed the knife she had and stabbed Sydney in the leg. "Lying bitch. That means I hate you. I own up to it."

Sydney screamed out in pain. "Okay, okay, I hate you! Damn, are you happy now?"

"Why couldn't you just let Lincoln be?"

"You don't love him!" Sydney shouted at her.

"What do you know about love?" Sonia asked.

"You have been cheating on him since the day you met him. I followed you. I know about the hotel suites and private dinners," Sydney snarled at her. "You don't deserve Lincoln."

"If you were such a good friend to him, then why didn't you say something to him."

"I didn't want to win him that way."

"You'll never win him," Sonia said. "You're not his type. You think, after all these years, he now magically wants you? Believe me, if he really wanted you, he would have made a move years ago. You're police trash. Your whole family is cops. Lincoln wants a woman with prestige and clout, not someone who can dismiss a parking ticket."

"You don't know him," Sydney said, though doubt had begun to seep into her mind.

"I'm the one who got him. What do you have?" Sonia laughed. "A moment? Ah, he'll forget about that. You'll always be number two."

A noise came from overhead. Sonia put tape on Sydney's mouth and went upstairs. When she got there, men from Sea Islands were waiting.

"We got your signal," one of the men said.

"Where is Lincoln?" Sonia asked.

174

"He should be arriving back in Sea Islands very soon. Their plane is in our atmosphere right now. I'm here to take you back on request of the queen."

"The queen," Sonia said with a smile.

"Are you ready to depart?"

Sonia thought about Sydney being tied up in her basement. "Yes, we can leave right now. I need to see Lincoln as soon as possible."

The Sea Islands men escorted her out to the door and into the helicopter.

In the basement, Sydney could hear the helicopter take off. She struggled to get loose but couldn't.

***

As the plane was landing, President McMillan addressed the nation on a live broadcast from the Oval Office. Agents Jones and Mitchell watched the broadcast on the plane's TV.

"At about oh seven hundred hours today, we captured King Jasani from the Sea Islands. Our goal as a nation is to reunite the Sea Islands with the United States of America. Step one is removing the wall, which we are in the process of doing, and step two is the surrendering of the Sea Islands back into the hands of our nation. Like all great wars that Americans have fought in, we only want to seek justice and provide the people of Sea Islands the best leadership possible. We understand that war is difficult and many people connected to you may die, but if your father, mother, or child is fighting on the American side, know that they are heroes in our world. God bless America."

When the broadcast ended, Agent Jones stared over at Agent Mitchell, confused by what she had just witnessed on TV.

"That's not the president," she said. "What the hell is going on?"

Agent Mitchell focused on the TV screen, thinking it was some kind of joke. When he realized it wasn't, he grabbed Lincoln by the neck and started choking him. Agent Jones pulled him off of Lincoln.

"We can't hurt him," she said. "Wherever we are, we might need him to get us back home."

"How is this even possible? That was Mayor McMillan. He's not the president of the United States."

Lincoln smirked. "Where did you think we were going, Mars?"

The plane landed.

"Did you see that? This plane just landed on autopilot," Agent Mitchell said, impressed by how smooth the landing was.

Agent Jones looked out the window, trying to see what was waiting outside for them when the cabin doors opened. She didn't see anything out of the ordinary, but she expected the worst.

"I don't trust it," she said as she stood Lincoln up. Agent Mitchell got Dalilah up. The steps automatically came out from within the plane as the cabin door opened.

The coast seemed clear as Agent Mitchell made his way down the stairs with Dalilah. Agent Jones quickly followed behind with Lincoln. As they reached the tarmac, the agents were shot with tranquilizer darts by long-range snipers. Within seconds, they were incapacitated and fell to the ground. Sea Islands royal council guards rushed onto the scene and took the handcuffs off Lincoln and then Dalilah.

Dalilah, who had been gagged for the entire trip, tried to get her lips back to normal. "Who are those people?" she asked Lincoln as the agents were carried away.

"What did they say to you?" he asked, curious about what she knew about the agents.

"I don't know. They seemed nice at the beginning. Then, when we got to the plane, things changed, and they treated me like I was a criminal. You, too. I thought they were going to kill you."

"I have to see where my family is and then figure out how to get my father back."

"I'll come with you. I need to call my father so that he knows I'm okay."

Leonard, King Jasani's chief counsel, was waiting for Lincoln at the car. Leonard assisted Dalilah into the car and closed the door. Then he pulled Lincoln far enough away that she couldn't hear their discussion. "How did you know it was me on the plane?" Lincoln asked.

"It has several hidden cameras throughout. Once we saw that the plane was on autopilot, we knew that something had gone wrong. I couldn't risk my men or you losing your life by giving them the advantage of knowing that we were waiting for them when the doors opened. The country would not look at me fondly if I got the prince killed."

"How bad is it, Leonard?" Lincoln asked, ending the chitchat.

Leonard sighed. "It's bad, your majesty. The American president is threatening to kill King Jasani if he doesn't sign over Sea Islands to him. Your mother and sisters are at the castle, waiting for you."

"How are they doing?"

"I would be lying to you if I painted any picture of the situation that seemed hopeful. Never in our history has a royal figure been kidnapped by another nation. The Americans are very unpredictable people when it comes to lives, especially black lives. The queen is taking it rather hard."

"What about Tia and Nicole?"

"Princess Nicole is quiet, but..." Leonard paused to make sure he said the right words.

Lincoln saw the hesitation. "Just spit it out. My feelings will not be hurt."

"Princess Tia is quite upset, and despite all the information against it, she seems to want to blame your coming back as the problem. The queen has sequestered her in her quarters."

"Let's go. I hope I can help. It needs to be quick. I have to get back to bring my wife and David back here."

"David is still alive?" Leonard asked, surprised. "But he's not with your wife."

"What are you talking about?"

"Your wife is on one of our planes heading back here now."

"How did that happen?" Lincoln asked.

"Your mother gave her a hair clip with a tracking device in it. We activated it when we never heard back from David. With her on one plane and you on the other, I assumed that David was dead."

Lincoln grimaced as he thought about Casey being shot right in front of him. "He was alive when I left. I need a team of people to go back and get him."

"Whatever you need, Prince Lincoln. I will get everything for your trip back."

"When will her plane be in?"

"In about an hour."

"Make sure someone brings her to me immediately."

"I will, sir, but for now, I need to get you to the queen," Leonard said as he walked over to the other side of the car and opened the door. Lincoln sat down in the backseat of the car. Leonard jumped in the passenger seat, and then the driver drove off.

***

In a dimly lit room down the hall from the Situation Room, Jasani was handcuffed to the table, his face in his hands. As President McMillan walked in, Jasani rose up to see who had come through the door. His face bore scars and lumps from the harsh beatings he had endured.

"You know, we can keep doing this forever," President McMillan said, looking at Jasani from the door.

"I'll never give you Sea Islands," Jasani said, his voice weak.

"That is really too bad. I wanted to at least spare your family, but I won't unless you sign the agreement. If you do, I will let you and your family live out this royal fantasy in Cuba. We have eyes on all the air travel in and out of Sea Islands."

Jasani's eyes perked up with concern.

"This can be over right now if you want it to be," President McMillan said, looking around at the cold walls the room. "Wouldn't you rather be somewhere else than here?"

"Kill me if you want. I will not surrender," Jasani said, staring President McMillan down.

President McMillan's chief of staff came to the door and signaled for the president to step out for a moment.

President McMillan stepped out of the room.

"Mr. President, I just got a confirmed message that two unidentified aircrafts have entered and landed in Douglasville."

"What do you mean by 'unidentified'?"

"We have no record of the flights leaving any airports or even leaving Douglasville. It's like they just popped up on our radar screen when they came into the airspace."

"Can we do anything about it?" President McMillan asked as he looked back in the room at Jasani.

"Not at this point. Our military forces are losing ground. They have more firepower than we expected. The Joint Chiefs are concerned by the number of soldiers we have lost so far. They are also concerned that if the Sea Islands troops push us back past the wall, they might want more United States land."

President McMillan was filled with fear. He didn't want to lose the war, and he definitely didn't want to concede more land in the process.

"What are they recommending?" he asked.

"They think we should surrender and try to work a new trade agreement."

"Surrender? Those chickenshits want these people running the world. I can't live in a world like this, where these black animals are in power. I refuse to work with them. You can't trust them. They all want to be kings."

The chief of staff saw the rage in the president's eyes. "Mr. President, this is a time to think strategically about our country's future."

"You think that man in there is going to be strategic if we let him go? He's going to come after my family, your family, and every other American family and destroy our world."

"What are you suggesting, Mr. President?" the chief of staff asked nervously, concerned about the response.

"I want our Air Force F-15E fighter pilots to start taking out all of their weapon facilities, and some of their national attractions, too."

"Mr. President, that would be a suicide mission for those pilots."

"Those pilots will be heroes. Set me up in a room with TV equipment and have them initiate the bombing of those sites. And have some guards bring him there. If his family loves him so much, let's see if they can handle seeing their king slowly die in front of the world."

"What about getting approval?"

"This is an executive order from the president. Get it done," President McMillan said, and then he walked off down the hallway.

The chief of staff stared into the room where Jasani was. Jasani looked back at him, and then the chief of staff rushed off in shame.

***

Lincoln walked into King Jasani's royal office. Ayanna saw her son and rushed to hug him. Tears of joy raced down her face.

"What can I do to get him back?" Lincoln asked.

Ayanna saw Dalilah creep up behind him. "Your father turned his back on us. That's a betrayal that will not go unnoticed in the future."

"Queen, I didn't know," Dalilah pleaded.

"Why would he do this at this time? What did you tell him?"

"I didn't tell him anything. He felt that you and the king had gone back on your word about me marrying the prince."

Ayanna looked at Lincoln.

"If it means getting my father back, I will commit to it. You have my word. Just get your father back to our table," he said to Dalilah. "I will contact him from the plane to confirm his allegiance."

"I will," she said, rushing off.

Ayanna grabbed Lincoln by the hand and guided him to another secret room where they could be alone. She sat down, and he sat across from her.

"Is everything alright?" he asked, knowing that it wasn't, especially with the sorrowful look on her face, which was now even more intense than when he had arrived.

"I have a team of soldiers going in to retrieve him." Her tears flowed down her face. "If they aren't able to get him, I think he will die in America."

"I'm going with them," Lincoln said, standing up. "When do they leave?"

"In an hour, but I can't risk losing both of you. This country will need a leader if Jasani doesn't make it back. I don't want to lose you again."

"I can't sit back and do nothing. My father needs me. I know I haven't known him my whole life, but if he was in my shoes, he'd be jumping on that plane to come get me. This is one risk that is worth taking. I'm sure none of these men have worked at the White House before."

"You have?"

"Yeah. I know the ins and outs of that building. If they have him anywhere, it's in the basement, near the PEOC. That's a room under the East Wing, the Presidential Emergency Operations Center. They definitely wouldn't be anywhere near the West Wing with a high-value hostage."

As Ayanna hugged him, someone knocked on the door.

"It's me," Nicole said. "Lincoln, you have a visitor."

"Sydney is back," he said with a smile. His mother smiled back at him. "Thanks for the hair clip. That saved her life; I'm sure of it. I'll be right back."

Lincoln walked out the door, and his mouth dropped when he saw Sonia standing there instead of Sydney. Sonia ran over to him and embraced him. He didn't move or react. People around the room, at the sight of him with a different woman than before, started to chatter amongst themselves.

"Where is Sydney at?" he asked as he surveyed the room.

"Who cares about her? I'm here."

"Did you hurt her?" he asked, knowing Sonia's presence was not coincidental.

"No. She came by and left. We talked. She understood that you love me more than anyone else."

Lincoln turned up his lip at her. "Why are you here? You turned on me."

"I had to save my family."

"You told me that your family disowned you ten years ago when you didn't marry that one guy."

"They were going to kill me. Besides, we both made it. I love you. We are meant to be together no matter where it is in the world. Where is this, exactly?" she asked, looking around at the castle walls and ceiling.

"You shouldn't be here," Lincoln said disapprovingly.

"And Sydney should?" Sonia retorted with meanness in her voice.

He turned away, not bothering to answer her question.

"I can't believe I gave you almost five years of my life for nothing. And you think that bitch is better than me? Are you fucking crazy?"

"It's not like that," Lincoln said, hoping she would calm down.

"Then what is it like?" Sonia asked as she jumped in his face. "Be a man for once, Lincoln."

"Sydney is my future. That's the truth. I was wrong trying to force a relationship with you because of status. We aren't meant to be together."

"So, you love her?"

"Madly."

Sonia slapped him across the face. The sound was so loud that everyone in the room stopped what they were doing. Even Tia, who was in another room, came over to see what had happened. She and Nicole both walked over to Lincoln and Sonia.

"Lincoln, is everything okay?" Nicole asked.

Sonia took issue with her butting in on their conversation. "Excuse me. We are having a private conversation," she said, turning up her nose at Nicole.

Nicole couldn't believe the attitude that Sonia was showing. Tia was in disbelief, too.

"Do you know that you cannot talk to royalty like that? Or even put your hands on us," Tia said arrogantly.

Sonia rolled her eyes. "Lincoln, who are these two women? Not more cheap hos."

Lincoln stepped between Tia and Nicole to block them from going after Sonia.

"Sonia, you need to leave," he said. "I will arrange for you to make it home safely."

"I'm not going anywhere until I get some answers."

Lincoln looked at the clock on the wall. "I have to go save my father. I can't deal with you right now."

"Your father? What is wrong with him?"

Lincoln was fed up with her snagging questions and attitude. "Guards," he said to the men by the door. They rushed over. Sonia stood there, trying to figure out what he was doing. "Please take her to a holding room or something. Make sure no one, and I mean no one, speaks to her."

The two guards grabbed her by the arms.

"Get your hands off me!" Sonia yelled. "Lincoln, you are going to pay for this."

The guards carried her away toward the family library down the hall. Lincoln turned to leave, but Tia jumped in his path.

"Who the hell was that witch?" she asked.

Lincoln looked at her, exhausted. "I really don't have the energy right now. I have to get on that plane to go bring our father home."

"How bad is it? Mother hasn't told us anything. This is like a nightmare," Tia said with pain on her face. "Are you responsible?"

"No," Lincoln said, dismissing any validity to her words. "And why would you think that?"

"This girl shows up. You come here with Sydney and lie that she's your wife. I don't know what's going on, but you are at the center of it. If my father dies because of you, I won't care if you're the king of the world, I will come after you."

Nicole stepped between them. "Tia, leave it alone. Lincoln didn't do this. The Americans have wanted that wall down for years, though they want to build the same type of wall to keep Mexico out. Don't turn this into something that it's not. I won't side with you."

"Then who did it?" Tia asked her sister.

"Not Lincoln. President McMillan and his family can't be trusted. I like Sydney, and I don't care if Lincoln is married to her or not. He probably said it to avoid being married to Dalilah."

Lincoln smirked.

"And who was that woman?" Tia asked.

"A long story. I promise the both of you, if I make it back, I will tell you everything that I can. But I will first have to go bring Sydney back here."

"I brought her sister here," Tia said with a smile. "I figured we all needed to be safe once the war started."

"What are you talking about?" Lincoln asked, confused by her statement.

"I found her sister and had her brought here. You didn't tell me she was a twin. At first, I was spooked out that they had the same name and everything else, but you have to realize everybody doesn't operate like normal humans."

"Please tell me you didn't." Lincoln froze, waiting for her response.

"She's right over there," Tia said, pointing to the corner of the room.

Lincoln's gaze wandered over to the corner. He saw her and smiled.

"I'll deal with that when I return."

He went back inside the room where he had left Ayanna.

"Is everything okay, son?" She smiled at him. "Are you sure you still want to go?"

Lincoln thought about everything that had transpired since he'd left the room fifteen minutes ago. He felt going to help save his father was a relief in comparison to dealing with Sonia and the Sydney of Sea Islands.

"Definitely. I just wanted to say bye, just in case I don't make it back."

"Don't you say that. I want you and Jasani back here. You promise me."

Lincoln looked in his mother's eyes. He didn't want to give her a promise that he couldn't fulfill, but he knew she needed some type of reassurance that everything would work out.

"I promise you."

Ayanna hugged him and kissed him on the cheek. "Hurry back," she said as he released her from their embrace and walked out of the room.

Chapter TWELVE

The president's chief of staff was in the Situation Room with the rest of the executive team. The room was in chaos, and the members of the executive team looked at the chief of staff as if he were joking.

"Has the president gone mad?" the secretary of defense asked as he stood up to go find him. "Where is he now?"

"He's on a live broadcast feed with Sea Islands royal council and queen," the chief of staff said, gritting his teeth. He knew the president had lost control, but he didn't know how to help the situation, aside from explaining what was currently happening.

"Doing what?" the vice president asked.

"He has the room heavily guarded and is threatening to kill King Jasani if he doesn't sign over the land rights of Sea Islands."

"The press is going to eat him alive," the director of homeland security said in disgust. "This is extremely embarrassing as a nation. We can't hold hostage the richest man in the world and threaten to kill him if he doesn't give up what is rightfully his. I thought we were done with this type of idiocrasy when Trump left office."

"Don't remind us of about his presidency," the secretary of state said with a smirk. "What is Sea Islands' position right now?"

The chief of staff frowned. "They have nuclear missiles ready to launch if we don't let him go."

"They don't want a nuclear war, nor do we," the secretary of state said.

"Does the president know something that we don't?" the vice president asked.

"No…" the chief of staff replied hesitantly.

"Spit it out!" the vice president shouted, irritated by the chief of staff's hemming and hawing. "We don't have time for delay."

"The president believes that by cutting body parts off the king over the live feed, he will get the queen of Sea Islands to give him what he wants."

"Damn!" the secretary of state said, slamming his hand down on the desk. "McMillan has gone mad. The Mad President is what he will be known as after this. If we all survive."

"He's your fucking best buddy. Why don't you go try to turn this around?" the chairman of the Joint Chiefs of Staff said to the vice president. "You two were Navy SEALs."

The vice president rolled his eyes at this. He hated that the chairman had brought that up. "I'll go talk to him. There must be a valid reason why Daniel is doing this."

"Yeah. Pissing off our country's neighbor. Canada and Sea Islands are close allies," the secretary of defense said, looking at everyone around the room. "The president is making us the meat in a possible sandwich."

The vice president got up and walked out of the room. When he got to where the President and Jasani were, he was confronted by the Secret Service agents guarding the door.

"I need to speak with the president," he said with authority.

"The president said to allow no one entry into this room until he walked out," the lead Secret Service agent said with stern aggression.

"Daniel! Daniel, let me in!" the vice president yelled from the hallway.

Surprisingly, the president came to the door and peeked out. "What do you want?"

"What's going on in there?" the vice president asked, trying to peek inside, but the door wasn't open enough for him to see anything.

"I'm close to saving America."

"What do you mean?"

"The queen of Sea Islands has agreed to all my terms. I will allow her and her family to leave respectfully and head to Cuba."

"The king agreed to that?"

"No, but she understands the severity of it all. America as we know it needs Sea Islands for its survival. Abe Lincoln, the worst president in our history, gave them something that he thought was nothing, and they grew it into what it is today. My legacy will be that of the president who made America great again."

"I'm sure they have a team on their way to retrieve him. That's in all military playbooks."

President McMillan smirked. "But they don't know how to get into the White House or down here. You just make sure to have the guys on the main floor ready for any intruders. Kill them on sight."

"Are you sure about this?"

"You've known me for over thirty years. I wouldn't be doing this if I wasn't sure. I was born to be president." President McMillan closed the door.

The vice president dragged himself back into the Situation Room. All eyes were on him as he entered.

"The president told me that the queen of Sea Islands has agreed to return ownership of the Sea Islands back to the United States in exchange for her husband's life."

"Something doesn't smell right," the secretary of defense said. "Outside of the king, they hold all of the cards. Why would you sacrifice your nation for your king? Their people won't go for that. The queen is setting a trap."

"But they don't know where we are, or him, for that matter. The White House is the most secure fortress in the world. You would have to know the entire layout to get into the building and then make it down here. That's an impossible mission."

***

Dalilah had finally reached her father. He was happy that she was safe, but he seemed unsure if that would continue to be the case.

"I want you to get on a flight this very minute. I don't want your safety to be in jeopardy."

"Father, are you hearing me? The prince has agreed to marry me. He gave me his word. His mother, the queen, was there to witness it."

Her father frowned. "That obligation is no longer yours. You do not need to wed him."

"Why not?"

The king looked at his watch. "Soon Sea Islands will be in a chaotic state, allowing me to take what the Americans don't want."

"What did you do, Father?"

"I secured your future. You can now marry anybody you please, within reason, of course. I have Shawn Douglas on his way here now."

"I want to marry Lincoln. I need you to fix whatever you have done!" Dalilah shouted at him. "I'm not marrying Shawn. The people of

Africa want me to marry Lincoln, not Shawn. Lincoln is the rightful heir to the throne. We can't just ignore that, Father."

"What's done is done. The king will be dead within the hour, and Lincoln will be crowned the new king, but what does he even know about running a monarchy? Nothing, and I will crush him. I don't need you in the picture when I do."

"I will never forgive you for this, Father!" Dalilah cried. "Just have our people in Washington, D.C., help Lincoln. He will need it to get back to Sea Islands after he gets his father."

The king grew angry at her demanding nature. "I expect to see you back here tomorrow. Leave that godforsaken place now."

***

Lincoln and about five Sea Islands special forces commandos parachuted onto a field about twenty miles from the White House. When they got on the ground, a white van with flowers on the sides was waiting on them. Once inside the vehicle, they started changing clothes.

"Have you heard from your African contact for our escape from D.C.?" one of the commandos asked.

Lincoln hated that he hadn't heard from Dalilah or her father, but he knew the guys in the van deserved the truth. "No. I think we are going to have to wing it. I understand if any of you guys want to turn around now. I have a plane for us to get back, but it won't be easy getting there."

"Are you sure about getting to the king?" another commando asked.

Lincoln smiled. "That part, I know."

All the commandos smiled at him.

"That's all I needed to know, Prince. If there's a way to get in, I'm finding a way out," one of the commandos said as he and his partners fist-bumped each other.

191

***

Still tied up in Sonia's basement, Sydney did all she could to break free of her restraints, but she couldn't. Though she was able to get the gag out of her mouth, her screams went unanswered. She wondered what had happened to Sonia and why she'd never returned. Considering what had happened over the last couple of days, she imagined that Sonia's disappearance had something to do with Lincoln. She just hoped that it was permanent. When she thought of Lincoln, the thought that they might not see each other again brought tears to her eyes.

"I don't know where you are, Lincoln. I am going to find you," Sydney said as she struggled to get loose again. Like the attempts beforehand, she couldn't get free.

***

Lincoln and the team of Sea Islands commandos were now dressed in business suits and carrying several bags containing their weapons as they drove into the parking garage on Seventeenth Street NW inside the Army and Navy Club building over at Farragut Square. After going down three levels, Lincoln had the driver park in the corner, facing out for a quick getaway.

Before jumping out, one of the commandos turned to Lincoln, curious about his knowledge of the place. It was a curiosity that all the other commandos had as well, but they were scared to ask because of Lincoln's status as prince.

"I'm not trying to be disrespectful, but how do you know all this information? This is not information the Americans share with Sea Islanders."

Lincoln saw the eyes of the men upon him. He knew that he couldn't tell them the truth, but he had to tell them something credible for them to have confidence that where he was leading them was actually real and would save the King.

"As you know, I didn't grow up in Sea Islands. I also wasn't a model citizen here. I acquired a lot of knowledge that probably isn't useful unless you're trying to save your father, who happens to be the king, or trying to kill the president of the United States. My friends have shown me plans and maps to get into the White House."

"Isn't it confidential information?" the same commando asked.

"Yes, but some people will tell you anything when they've had a lot to drink. This access point was created in 1911 so that President Taft could freely go from the West Wing to here without people knowing. When Reagan was president, they demolished and rebuilt this building and cut off the access to the tunnel, but the tunnel is still there."

"So, there is a chance that when we go in here, we can be ambushed?" another commando asked.

"Like I said before, if you don't trust me or the plan, I respect you being honest and not coming, but as for me, I'm going in there and bringing my father back."

The men looked at each other, contemplating what they should do.

Lincoln opened his car door. "I don't have time to waste. I know where they are hiding him, and that's a promise. It's in a room under the East Wing. The room is called the PEOC, the Presidential Emergency Operations Center. It's not going to be easy getting there. Some of us might not make it out. We're less than a third of a mile away right now."

Lincoln got out of the car, went over to a manhole in the opposite corner of the garage, and opened it. He started to go down the ladder when the commandos came over to him.

"We want to have some fun, too," one of the commandos said to him with a smile.

"Can't have a party without people," Lincoln said.

He climbed down three more levels, finally reaching an opening where with a door. He got off the ladder, and the commandos joined him.

Lincoln took out a plastic explosive device and placed it on the door. All the men stepped away as he detonated it. When they opened the door, everyone was prepared to fire back, but no one was on the other side.

Lincoln and the commandos quickly ran through the tunnel under Lafayette Park, towards Madison Place. As they got to the tunnel door entrance to the Treasury Building, they stopped. One of the commandos looked at the steel blast-resistant door. He shook his head in disappointment as he looked up and saw the small camera staring at him.

"Damn. Let's get ready. They know we are here now. Let's use C4 and blast the door off."

"We have about five minutes to get my father out," Lincoln said to the team.

One of the commandos placed two sticks of C4 on the door, and all the men moved far away from it. Immediately after the blast went off, gunfire rained down on Lincoln and the commandos from the security team in the Treasury Building.

Using multiple hand grenades, the team cleared the way, but it didn't prevent two of the commandos from being killed in the tunnel. Lincoln's left arm was grazed by a bullet. He and the three commandos left made it across to the East Wing. Once inside the White House, they faced more resistance and fighting. They also lost one more person as they headed under the East Wing to the PEOC.

***

President McMillan heard all the noise outside the PEOC room. He opened the door to find out what was going on from the Secret Service agents blocking entry into the room.

"Do I hear gunshots?" he asked.

"Mr. President, I advise you to stay inside until we have a way for us to take you to a more secure location," said one of the agents.

"What is happening?" President McMillan asked, mad at the agent for not just spitting out the details.

"Mr. President, all we know at this time is that some rebel forces have breached the Treasury Building and are now heading down here. We have started shutdown protocols, but I advise you to take shelter inside the PEOC. You should be safe."

President McMillan looked back at Jasani and the TV monitor. He closed the door and ran over to Jasani. He pulled his gun out and put it to Jasani's head. On the TV monitor was Ayanna.

"You fuckin' tricked me, you bitch!" President McMillan said, cocking the gun.

Jasani was too dazed to realize what was happening, but Ayanna saw her life with him flash in front of her eyes. From the president's hysteria, she knew that Lincoln and the team had made it at least that far. But with the president being out of control and holding a gun to Jasani's head, she knew it was only a matter of seconds before he got angry enough to shoot him.

"I promise I didn't. Check your email. I signed it, and everything is yours," she said. "Please don't kill him." Ayanna prayed that the president checking his email would buy Lincoln a little more time to save Jasani.

"Then who are these people coming to get me down here?"

Ayanna looked at the clock on her wall and then at Jasani. She knew her lying was coming to an end if Lincoln wasn't able to get him out soon.

With one hand, President McMillan checked his email account. He saw the attached document labeled "Signed Sea Islands Agreement." He smiled as he opened it. Right when it opened and he saw the words "Go Fuck Yourself!" Lincoln burst through the door and shot him in the arm.

Thinking President McMillan was down, Lincoln went to get his father free so that they could escape. One of the two surviving commandos came into the room.

"We have to get above ground to escape," the commando said, looking at Jasani and Lincoln.

"Grab him," Lincoln said, pointing at the president. "He's our lottery ticket out of here."

The commando grabbed President McMillan, and they made their way up the stairs to the East Wing. Gunshots and bombs flew everywhere as they made it to the White House front lawn. Once the Secret Service and the US military saw that President McMillan was a hostage, the shooting stopped. Lincoln, Jasani, and the last Sea Islands commando, who had President McMillan, jumped into a government-registered SUV and barreled through the White House gates and onto the streets. Behind them were about half of all government and police officers in Washington, D.C.

It took about thirty minutes for Lincoln to drive them to Potomac Airfield in Fort Washington, Maryland. They quickly jumped out of the SUV and onto the plane that was waiting for them. The government and police officers arrived and attempted to stop them from liftoff, but the plane took off and disappeared in the sky.

As they reached altitude, Lincoln went over to his father and realized that he had been shot somewhere along the getaway. Though he wasn't dead, blood was gushing his body like water from a faucet. Lincoln held his father as the plane flew to Sea Islands.

The second-shift prison guard let Agent Jones and Mitchell meet in a hallway downstairs. The hallway was the separation point for the women and men sections of the prison. The guard only let them meet because Agent Jones had promised to do some sexual favors for him later. She had only made the promise because she didn't plan on being around to fulfill it.

"I think we can make it out of here," Agent Mitchell said.

"What is here? What is this place?" Agent Jones asked, trying to wrap her head around where they were.

Agent Mitchell shrugged. "I don't know, but I'm not sticking around to be somebody's lab rat."

She glanced around curiously. "Don't you think it's odd that all the people running things are black?"

"This isn't my country; I know that much. I'm going to go back to where I'm from. Are you with me?"

Agent Jones looked around again. Though she knew it was best to stay with her partner, a part of her wanted to stay longer and find out what this black environment was really about.

"Of course," she said with doubt in her voice.

"Tonight we leave during the changeover of the guards. It will be a piece of cake. Get outside, take a car, and get back to Chicago."

"You think a car is going to get us back?" she asked, thinking his logic was off.

"You think this is like another country or planet? Please. I know Florida when I see it. This is some type of mind-altering cult shit. We just have to get out of it."

With his father's blood covering his clothes, Lincoln slowly walked out of the emergency room exit at Sea Islands General Hospital. Ayanna, Nicole, and Tia were nervously waiting for him.

"Is he going to make it?" Ayanna asked.

"How bad is it?" Tia asked.

Lincoln stared at all three of them. "The doctors don't know. He's in a coma. They removed the bullet from his lungs, but the..." He paused, not wanting to say the rest.

"What is it, Lincoln?" Nicole asked, breaking her silence.

"The cancer is spreading even more," Lincoln said, in tears.

Ayanna looked at Lincoln, stunned by what he had just said. "Cancer? Jasani has cancer? He didn't tell me. Are you sure?"

"The doctors confirmed it."

"Oh, no," Ayanna said as she fainted in her daughters' arms.

Tia and Nicole carried her over to the nearest open seat. Lincoln didn't know what else to say, so he went over to the window and looked out. Tia left her mother and sister to go over to him. She stood next to him for a couple of seconds before he looked at her.

"You know, I want to thank you for saving my...I mean, our father. I hope you understand what this means right now."

"What does it mean?" Lincoln asked, hoping that she would expound on what she was talking about.

"You're the new king. And if Father doesn't live, you will be king permanently."

"Damn," Lincoln said. "Don't talk like he's not going to make it."

"I know it's a lot, but Sea Islands can't have a gap in leadership. We have to rebuild our wall and show the world that we are not weak. Even King Tanana, Dalilah's father, has to pay for turning his back on us. And the

Americans will not like that we have their president. We will need to strike our enemies quickly and decisively."

"I never asked for this," Lincoln said, wishing he wasn't the one to take the throne.

"You know what Father would say to you right now?" she asked with a big smile through her tears.

"What?" Lincoln asked, clueless.

"When everything seems to be going against you, remember that the airplane takes off against the wind, not with it."

"Sydney! I got to go get her," he said.

"Where is she, anyway?" Tia asked with her brow raised. "That twin of hers doesn't even know about her. She's actually kind of weird."

"Sydney doesn't have a twin. Just have that woman go home. I'll be back soon." Lincoln rushed off.

***

The prison guard changeover started at 8:30 PM. When one of the black female guards, who had just started her shift, walked by Agent Jones' cell, the agent grabbed her and broke her neck, killing her. Agent Jones quickly undressed the guard and put on her uniform. She then went to the prison control center and cut off the power to all the cell doors throughout the prison. Seeing that their cells were open and they could escape, the prisoners rushed the other guards and made their way out of the prison.

***

When Lincoln boarded the plane, Sonia was there with a guard next to her. He took a seat by the door across from her. The Sea Islands national security director and his two assistants hopped on the plane with President McMillan, who was in cuffs. The president's leg was wrapped up in bandages after the surgery to remove the bullet from his leg. He frowned at Lincoln.

"I'm coming back to get you," President McMillan said as one of the assistants moved him to the back of the plane, far away from Lincoln.

"King Lincoln, the two other prisoners escaped," the national security director said with shame, like it was his own fault.

"Damn," Lincoln said, balling up his fist. Then he thought about it and chuckled. "That's a different type of prison, but find them. I want them to pay for what they did to Casey." He stared over at Sonia.

"So, your father is dead?" she asked.

"No."

"Then why did he address you as king?"

"My father is in a coma. He's going to make it."

"And if he doesn't, you'll be king permanently," Sonia said with a smile. "Sounds like a win-win for you."

He stared at her like she was crazy. "What are you talking about?"

"Just a few days ago, you told me you wanted to be legendary. I guess some dreams can come true."

"You think I asked for all this?" he said, rolling his eyes at her.

"It's still not too late for us," Sonia replied, batting her eyes at him.

"I just need to go back and get Sydney and see if I can get David."

"Did they have David at that hospital in the basement? If so, he is lost. I wouldn't try that even if I was stupid. You really giving up on us for her?" Sonia fumed.

Lincoln stared into the distance as the plane took off down the runway. He was going to avoid answering her question, but then he remembered her statement about him being a man. He turned to face her.

"She is the one. I apologize for everything I did wrong in our relationship. I do love you. That's the God's honest truth. The difference is that I'm totally in love with her. Have been since I met her. I just never had that moment of clarity to realize it until we made it here. I don't want to live without her."

"So, what's going to happen with me?" she asked, thinking it would be something bad.

"Nothing."

She raised her brow at him, thinking he was lying. "I'm no dummy."

"No, for real. I really want you to be happy. I'm letting you go back to your life."

"And picking up Sydney to take back with you to be queen." Smoke came out of her nostrils at the thought of Sydney being crowned queen. "You got to be kidding me."

Lincoln got up, walked into the master suite, and closed the door.

***

Back in Sonia's basement, Sydney made it over to a wall and started rubbing the chair against it, hoping to break the ropes. The gold hair clip fell out of her hair and slid under a table.

***

Agent Jones and Mitchell stole a car and drove off down the road. They saw a sign saying for I-95 North to Atlanta, and they swerved onto the on-ramp.

"If you are right, we'll take a flight from Atlanta to Chicago," Agent Jones said, still contemplating whether she should be leaving an environment where black people were in charge.

***

As the plane landed, Sonia secretly sent a text message to the police: "I'm being held against my will. Track my phone."

In the black SUV, Lincoln had President McMillan dropped off at the place of Sarah's husband's black girlfriend. When the girlfriend opened up the door, she jumped into the president's arms, only to be rebuffed by him. He stared at her like she was the scum of the earth.

"Nigger, what are you doing?" he asked her with his nose turned up in the air.

"Daniel, what the fuck you call me?" she said and started punching him.

Lincoln laughed as the driver took off.

As they pulled into Sonia's subdivision, Lincoln could tell she was a little too calm about what was happening. He looked out the car window but didn't see anything. The car pulled up to the house.

"Are you sure you don't know where Sydney might be?" he asked before she got out of the car.

She smiled at him. "No. Have a nice life in jail."

As she rushed into the house, Lincoln saw the police converging on the property and trying to surround them. The national security director and his assistants fired at the officers and did everything to protect Lincoln.

Sonia went inside the house and down to the basement with a butcher knife, which she grabbed off the kitchen counter. Her eyes showed her evil intent as she made her way downstairs. When she saw that Sydney had escaped, she raced back upstairs and out the front door.

The driver pulled away, speeding down the street from the police cars. When Lincoln noticed Sydney running towards them, waving her hands, he made the driver stop to get her. Sydney jumped in, and they rushed off.

Sonia was pissed to the high heavens that Lincoln and Sydney were together again. From the smalls of her back, she pulled out a book titled the 'The History of Sea Island.'

"I'm going to make you and her pay, Lincoln. That's a promise and believe me I will see you again." Sonia headed back down to the basement.

Back in the basement, while cleaning up the mess that Sydney had made when escaping, Sonia saw the gold hair clip.

"I wonder what this is for?" she asked, examining it closely.

***

It took a lot of evasive driving and near-crashes, but Lincoln and Sydney made it back to the airplane. The chase was so tight that when they jumped on the airplane, they didn't even have time to buckle up before it jetted off back to Sea Islands.

When the national security director approached Lincoln on the plane and called him "King," Sydney looked at Lincoln with sorrow.

"Your father died," she said with tears in her eyes.

"No. I think he's going to make it. That is my title until he comes out of his coma."

"So, what happened?"

"President McMillan kidnapped and tortured him. We went and rescued him, but he was shot during our escape."

"I see I missed a lot," Sydney said snuggling up next to him. "I don't want to leave your side again."

"I don't want you too, either." Lincoln smiled.

"I guess Sea Islands is now our new home," Sydney said smiling back at him.

"Are you sure you want this?" Lincoln asked.

"As long as I'm with you that's all that matters. This is your destiny. I will be by your side no matter as long as you want me to be your queen."

Lincoln leaned in and kissed her. "You think I can one day be a great King? This world is so different than the one we just left."

"But it a world where black people have power and a say in the world. Is this what we always ask for?" Sydney looked into his eyes.

"Yeah, you're right."

"People will love you. Your sisters seem like they like you. Black unity is beautiful."

Lincoln smirked. "I do want to meet this cousin Shawn. I'm sure he feels a certain way about me being in the picture."

Sydney kissed him. "You will someday be the greatest King ever in Sea Islands."

"With my Queen anything will be possible."

Sydney remembered the gold hair clip and reached in her hair. She freaked out when she noticed it was gone. She turned to Lincoln.

"I lost the hair clip your mother gave me."

"I'm sure it's no big deal," Lincoln said holding her hands.

***

At Sea Islands General Hospital, the doctor walked over to Ayanna and her daughters.

"Is he going to be okay?" Tia asked him before he could even get a word out.

The doctor looked the three of them in the face. "I'm not sure he's going to make it through the night," he said. "We have the best specialist in the world treating him right now."

"You have to save my father," Nicole said. "He's the king."

204

"I know. Like I said, we are doing the best we can. I'll be back in a couple of hours to give you another update." The doctor turned and walked away.

Nicole looked at her mother. "Is Lincoln ready to be king?"

"If it comes to that, your brother will have to be ready."

Tia got a phone call. She looked at the caller ID and saw it was a call coming in from Kenya. She walked off down the hallway and answered.

"Hello," she said, wondering who was calling.

"Hello, Princess Tia. This is King Tanana."

"Bye. You didn't even want to help my father when he needed you."

"Hold on. I understand your feelings, but this call isn't about emotions. This is a call about power and money."

"I don't have time for this," Tia said angrily.

"I heard about your father being in a coma."

"He's going to make it."

"What if he doesn't?"

"My brother will be crowned king."

"You think he can rule Sea Islands like your father?"

Tia exhaled. "What are you getting at?"

"I'm coming for Sea Islands. Your people will not stand for an outsider as a ruler for long. But there is a solution to that."

Tia rolled her eyes. "Keep talking."

King Tanana smiled. "You can rule Sea Islands while I preside over it as king in name only."

"And what about my family?"

"Nothing will change. Lincoln will be exiled to Cuba."

"That's a change right there." She smirked. "You want me to help bring down my brother. My mother would be destroyed."

205

"Like I said, I'm coming for Sea Islands if your father doesn't survive. You have to decide: do you want to be on the losing side or the winning one. Your cousin Shawn has already decided to marry my daughter Dalilah. She's heading back here now."

"What?" Tia asked.

"If your father doesn't make it, I will need an answer from you within twenty-four hours. After that, you will go down with the ship. Bye."

As King Tanana hung up, Tia held the phone, thinking about what he had said.

***

As the plane landed, Lincoln and Sydney got off. From the top step, they saw Dalilah waiting on the tarmac. They slowly walked down the stairs. When they reached the tarmac, Dalilah approached them.

"My father is coming after you," she said. "I can help you defeat him."

"How?" Lincoln asked.

Sydney followed with her own question: "Why?" She was suspicious of Dalilah's intentions.

***

Outside the old abandoned Manteno State Hospital was Sonia, dressed in a black sweat suit with a baseball cap on. She held a flashlight making her way down some stairs that led to a door that looked old and dusty. She knocked on it. After a few minutes, a couple of agents came to the door with their guns drawn.

"What are you doing back here?" the agent asked. "What happened to Agent Jones and Mitchell?"

"I'm here to help. And I know where they are too."

"Help who," the agent replied back.

Sonia smiled. "The both of us."

"Why?"

"Strictly revenge," Sonia said holding the gold hair clip in one hand and the book in the other.

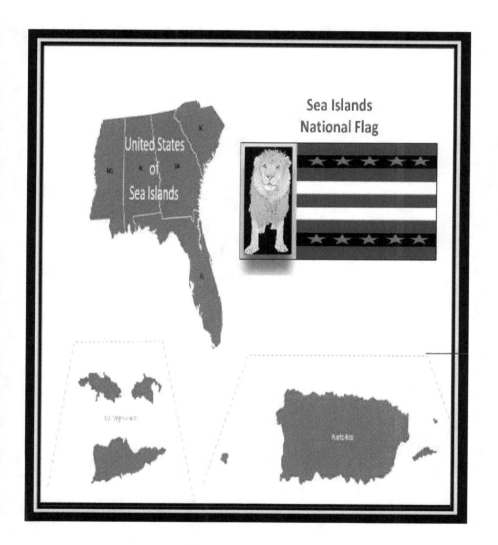

Sea Islands
National Flag

United States
of
Sea Islands

CPSIA information can be obtained
at www.ICGtesting.com
Printed in the USA
FSHW021131251120
76150FS